About the Book

This is the story of Angus MacLeod, his grandson, Tor, and the land they live on. The MacLeod farm straddles the gently rolling crest of one of Virginia's Blue Ridge Mountains and spreads out its beautiful patchwork of fields and sheep meadows almost as far as the eye can see.

But this story is set in today's world, which means that the MacLeod land—like land everywhere else today—is in terrible danger. For when a system of federal parks and highways is planned to run along the heights of this very chain of mountains, Tor and Angus MacLeod realize that they may be forced to sell their farm and to lose the old place where their family has had its roots for generations.

How old Angus MacLeod and young Tor struggle to save a part of their heritage from the implacable jaws of the machine age makes a powerful story whose relevance and urgency all young readers will understand.

The MacLeod Place

by
William H. Armstrong

Coward, McCann & Geoghegan, Inc.
New York

The author gratefully acknowledges permission to reprint,
on p. 189, From THE HILLS BEYOND by Thomas Wolfe (Harper & Row).

 Published simultaneously in Canada by
Longmans Canada Limited, Toronto.
SBN: GB-698-30471-3
SBN: TR-698-20193-0
Library of Congress Catalog Card Number: 72-83601
Printed in the United States of America

The
MacLeod
Place

The race is not to the swift,
Nor the battle to the strong,
Nor bread to the wise,
Nor riches to the intelligent,
Nor favor to men of skill;
But time and chance happen to them all.

Ecclesiastes 9:11

❧ One ❧

The school bus, its radiator steaming from the steep pull up the rutted, winding mountain road, choked and lumbered to a halt. The driver growled aloud to himself, "If they ever decide to finish that highway along the mountaintop, all these cussed up-and-down roads will be straightened out and surfaced so the bottom won't fall out of them at spring mud time."

The large homemade mailbox in front of which the bus stopped showed the weathered stencil of the name MacLeod. There could be faint doubt that among the little girls on the bus, their noses pressed against the windows, at least one, taking in the gable roof of the mailbox with its shingles, door and hinges all proportioned the right size, did not say, "I wish I had that for a dollhouse." Or some boy, with a new pup, measuring its size with his mind's eye, could see it set on the ground by a kitchen door for a doghouse.

"You're breaking the rule again," the bus driver broke off talking to himself and called back to the boy who was out of his seat and halfway down the aisle before the bus had stopped.

The boy did not answer. He fingered the middle

horn button of his yellow-and-black plaid Mackinaw and shuffled his heavy boots to balance himself. The strap of his canvas book satchel creased itself in the broad lamb's fleece collar of his jacket. The tin lunch box in his free hand managed to bang against the corner of each seat he passed.

As the bus driver reached for the lever to open the door, he scowled. "What's the big rush all the time?"

If the boy had answered, it would have taken too long. The driver would not have understood anyway. For to hear a ten-year-old boy say, "I'm in a hurry to get to the MacLeod place," would have only made the driver scowl more. It would also have made the children on the bus laugh and yell, "You're silly, Torm MacLeod."

But Tor MacLeod knew his two worlds. There was the outside world of the school bus and the town at the foot of the mountain, and school bells, blackboards, and noise, and rows of desks and teachers. There was pushing in line at recess and fights with bad words and sticks. And Tor MacLeod's outside world took in the big town, far away, more than a hundred miles, out of sight of the mountains, where he had gone to live. Where there was nothing to do. And after school or all day long somebody would be asking, "What'll we do now?" Where there was nothing to walk on but hard gray cement, and nothing to see but walls and windows; or maybe on Saturday or Sunday go to a park that wasn't as big as Grandpa's night pasture. And night pastures are small so the cows won't be too far from the barn to come when you call them in the morning, so you won't have too far to tramp in the dew-soaked grass to bring them.

The other world of Tor MacLeod was the world of Grandpa Angus MacLeod. It was the night pasture and the day pasture, the pie-shaped field and the cold-spring lot, the mountain pasture that rolled up against the north cliffs, where pines and mountain laurel grew right out of the rocks, and Grandpa called the cliffs the Hanging Gardens.

This was the world that Grandpa called the middle fields. "Midway between earth and heaven," he said, "as close to heaven as a man ought ever want to be." Sometimes Tor MacLeod would get to thinking that Grandpa MacLeod had made it all himself, just like God, and separated it out the way he liked it; and sometimes Tor was certain Grandpa would have to change the world he had made. He never talked about it much to Grandpa, for it made Grandpa mad. Sometimes he asked his grandmother why Grandpa was so old-fashioned, and his grandmother would smile and say, "He wants you to have a lot of exciting things to do when you grow up, like changing things to make a real modern farm."

But any talk of change riled Grandpa. Like if he'd heard the bus driver growling about the highway and new roads, he would have said, "Now the first MacLeod made it up this mountain in 1782 without a road at all. And a lot of MacLeods have made it up and down since. What's so bad about a little spring mud? The earth heals her own scars pretty fast if they're only mud. But if you skin her surface and rip into her bowels and then try to heal her up with a plaster of asphalt or concrete, she's scarred forever."

Tor was certain that's what his grandpa would have said to the bus driver. For that's what he had said to some men who had come along the mountain, measuring and driving stakes with numbers on them in the fields last summer. They had said they were surveying for a map. But Grandpa was suspicious that they might be surveying for the Skyland Parkway, which now and then rumor had extending along the whole mountaintop. So he lectured the men about how a highway scarred the earth. Then when they had been gone a long time, Tor noticed that their stakes had disappeared from the fields.

Grandpa had gotten awfully mad, too, when a stranger came asking about crops. "A study by the government," he said, "to determine the productivity of mountain farms in the area."

Grandpa Angus MacLeod had stopped his rocking chair dead still for a long time and gazed out over the fields a long time before he spoke. When his bootheels began to tap the stone floor of the porch, Tor knew he was "mighty vexed," as the boy's grandmother said.

"Seven generations of MacLeods, men, women, and children, tamed this land and prayed and cursed it into fruitfulness—or producing or whatever you want to call it.

"You'll have to get your answers somewhere else," Angus said without rising as the stranger left.

Tor MacLeod liked the things he could do in Grandpa's world, though. There was a lot of everything to do and not too much of any one thing for too long, and this was right for a boy. Much better than using fingers to roll spitballs or throw chalk or push people or play with the horn buttons on his jacket that were already buttoned.

Once off the school bus, there was kindling wood to split for the cookstove and the wood corner to fill for the fireplace. Corn to shell for the chickens. Calves and sheep to throw hay to out of the high barn loft, and hay and leather to smell in the barn. Barn doors to open. Horses to let out, and tails and manes to watch flying in the wind as the horses raced to the creek to drink. And in winter the hole in the ice to keep chopped open. Gates to open for the cows. Gates to swing on, and "Always latch after you," Grandpa said. Straw bedding to put under pigs; and in spring, lambs to carry in to warm behind the kitchen stove.

Tor MacLeod barely touched the step of the school bus with one foot and planted the other with such a giant step in the spring mud that he almost lost his balance and fell. Two little girls clapped their hands against the bus window and yelled, "Good-bye, Torm. Don't fall in the mud, Torm."

Tor didn't look back or pretend to hear. Shep, the farm dog, was waiting by the mailbox, as he had been doing, always at exactly the right time, since Tor had started to ride the seven miles to school at the foot of the mountain. Here too the boy and dog waited together in the morning. And not until the bus door folded securely behind the boy did Shep return to the kitchen door or find his senior master, Angus MacLeod, at the barn.

Tor gave the dog a hug and ran his fingers through the heavy black-and-white winter hair that was just beginning to dull and loosen—another sign of spring.

"For four years I've told them to call me Tor, that I don't like the name Torm. And for four years and spite, some silly girl or stupid boy who's looking for a fight calls me Torm. But we don't care now, do we, Shep?" And Shep agreed with a wag of his tail and by bumping his head against the boy's tin lunch pail, trying to walk closer.

"We don't care now, and that didn't hurt, did it, Shep?" Tor MacLeod ran his free hand up over the white nose of Shep and let it rest just below the liquid-brown eyes. "There never was a better name for a real dog like you than Shep, was there, Shep? With hounds it's different. They can have fancy names like Blue Boy and Tennessee Belle 'cause they ain't smart like you."

Except for the pause to comfort Shep, Tor's wide strides were hurrying him toward the great slab of stone "bigger than a dining-room table," his grandpa Angus said, "that a four-horse team had dragged from the high pasture and put in place before the kitchen door when the high pasture was still a wilderness, seven generations of MacLeods ago."

And all these generations had caused Tor to have the name he didn't like. Even Grandpa MacLeod had finally settled for Tor. But sometimes when he was stern, he said, "Torm! Torm MacLeod! I told you not to use my sharp ax." Or yelled across the meadow, "Torm! How many times do I have to tell you not to loiter by the creek when you're fetching the cows?" But he never tired of explaining why Torm was a name to make a MacLeod proud.

"Not a Torm MacLeod this side of Glenelg, Scotland," he would say. "And the last one died at the Battle of Worcester, in 1651, when more than seven hundred MacLeods were killed, the whole clan almost wiped out."

Tor knew the story so well it flashed through his mind in just about the time it took to put his book satchel and lunch box on the great stone step and say "Shut up!" to the two Bluetick foxhounds who raised themselves on their front legs, from where they lay asleep in the sun, and sent one long musical bay rolling echoless over the fields that sloped south to the sun.

"Nothing but Rory, Hugh, Angus, Mohr, and Ennis for generations," Grandpa would repeat always in that order, "until your own pa was born. And I said to your grandma, who was partial to the name Logan, from her family, 'The first MacLeod was named Torm, and I want that name for my first son. You can name the next one Logan.' So your pa was named Torm. Then when you came along, your pa said, 'I want my boy named for me.' Your mother said it was clannish, but your pa won out. And I said, 'There are no junior MacLeods.' Every MacLeod is his own man, so that's why you are Torm MacLeod, the Second."

Tor admitted to himself, when he was walking alone in the fields or watching the sunset, that he was proud of his name. For when his father had gone away to war in Europe, he had written back in a letter to Tor's mother: "Tell Tor that everybody gets my name wrong. It's been typed Storm on orders so often that now all the soldiers in my company call me Captain Storm."

Then word came that his father was dead and would not come home from war. And Uncle Logan would not come either. Uncle Logan never married. He had gone to war young. He flew so many missions and logged so many victories that people in his squadron called him Logger Logan.

After all this had happened, Tor waited for the long weeks to end when he didn't cry at night. He kept still the many months that passed until he could talk without choking on a big lump in his throat and feeling sick to his stomach.

When the days no longer ended in quiet, when only the crackling of dry logs or spewing sap in the great fireplace at the end of the kitchen broke the heavy silence of the endless nights before bedtime, he learned to breathe again without hurting. When his mother and grandmother, Una Logan MacLeod, and Grandpa talked about Torm and Logan "when they were little boys," Tor finally learned to listen without getting up to punch at the fire or stretch out on the bearskin rug with Shep so they couldn't see him cry.

This was when he had come to be proud of his name. And when he was ready, it came to him. So one night as Grandpa sat before the fire and talked of other things—plowing the pie-shaped field, seedtime, new calves, and how the golden eagle had returned a third year to nest in the Hanging Gardens—Tor leaned against his chair, wrapped a child's hand halfway around the gnarled knuckles of his grandfather's hand, looked up into eyes lined by sorrow, wisdom and weather, and said, "I'm glad my name is Torm. If Pa was Torm and I'm Torm, and I'm alive, then I'm just like Pa, I guess."

⚜ Two ⚜

The incident with the girls when he left the bus had started Tor on this thinking about things. "Sometimes people say things that get a person's hackles up. Don't they, Shep?" He rolled the woodshed door back on its groaning rusty rollers and motioned with his hand for Shep to enter.

Realizing at once that he was not doing things the way he had planned, he continued speaking as Shep stood wagging his tail. "This isn't where I was headed. It's lambing time and I was going to the barn to see if anything happened today. That's why I didn't stop in the kitchen for soup and bread and jam. Come on, Shep. Let's go to see if there're new lambs in the shed. Grandpa's Black-faced Highlands probably dropped a dozen."

On the way to the low-roofed shed, which ran the whole length of the barn on the south side, Tor was still thinking about his two worlds, which nobody except him and Grandpa really understood, and their understanding had its differences. For Tor's grandpa it was a dreaming backward, a determination to keep this mountain kingdom untouched by the outside world. For Tor it was a dreaming forward to the day when there would be tractors to ride and three moldboard plows on one hitch to plow a whole field in half a day, like Mr. Hillyer's farm down over the slope of the mountain. But even if Grandpa wouldn't change, this was better than the world outside.

When his mother had married a nice man named Dr. Charlton and gone to live in the city, Tor had gone too. Except for the year his pa was killed and Uncle Logan was lost, last year in the city had been his most terrible year. Nothing to do after school every day and all day Saturday and Sunday. Never able to wear a Mackinaw with horn buttons and brogan boots with brass buckles. Nothing but lace-up, polished shoes, Sunday clothes on weekdays, and a dark-blue overcoat that reached down to his knees like the one the preacher wore at the church at the foot of the mountain. The preacher who never smiled.

So about March of this awful year Tor had started marking off the days on the calendar till June, when he would go to Grandpa's house to stay all summer.

"Remember last summer, Shep? How you licked my face when I got out of Mother's car? And then you ran around the car three times, jumping and barking, and licked my face some more?

"Remember, Shep? There never was such a summer, and a few more months and there'll be another. This year I'll be bigger and can do more things."

Tor unlatched the barnyard gate and rode it around to where its age sag brought the bottom plank against the ground. It rolled up a scroll of mud and stopped.

There he seated himself on the top plank, hooked the heels of his brass-buckled brogan boots behind the third plank down, and sat facing the sun—a sun warm enough to start the sap of life running in a tree.

"If there were any new lambs, they would be baa-baaing all over creation and we could hear them from here," Tor said to Shep, remembering he was still hurrying to the barn. And Shep moved from the center of the open gate, where he had stood with ears cocked ready to keep something out or something in, to sit on his haunches and look up into the face of the boy.

"Remember, Shep, how Grandpa said the hogs even grunted cheerful-like when I came back? And all two hundred of Grandpa's Black-faced Highland ewes danced around me in a circle, they were so happy? I knew he was only spoofing and that the sheep were just skittish because they had forgotten me and I was a stranger. All animals are skittish about strangers—especially sheep and young cattle.

"Remember how Mother stayed a week to be sure I didn't get kicked by a horse or fall out of the hayloft or something, and then she came to visit often because I couldn't stand to go back to the hot cement city to see her? And how she always brought me city things like white shirts and box games and a bathing suit? And whoever went swimming in the creek in a bathing suit? And I said bring me a barlow knife with two blades and a gimlet, or a calf halter, or some strap leather, or twenty feet of half-inch hemp rope, or a whetstone small enough to carry in my back pocket.

"Wasn't it funny that she didn't know better? Even if she had been a town person before she married my father, she'd lived here long enough to know the kinds of things a man needs.

"Well, I got the answer to why she didn't know better, around August, when I used to crawl out my window and listen to what they were saying about my going back to winter with Ma and my stepfather. Seems my stepfather had always lived in a town, and he was the one picking out all them useless things for me.

"When Grandma heard they were coming here to spend the whole month of August, she said Dr. Charlton was used to big vacation places and hotels and travel and wouldn't last out a week up here where there's nothing but quiet.

"Grandpa said, 'Let him try it, might give him a world of rest.' Said that since he was one of those mind doctors or psycho-something, he might learn that there ain't no medicine for the mind like land and mountain quiet.'"

Tor MacLeod shifted his weight just enough not to lose his balance but to pull a bone-handled barlow knife from somewhere deep in his corduroy pants pocket. He opened the small blade and rubbed both sides of it across the palm of his hand the way his grandpa always did the butcher knife when he sliced ham at the dinner table.

The weathered shavings that he began to whittle from the top plank of the gate fell too close to Shep's upturned nose, so Shep shook himself and moved back a foot or two.

"You know, Shep, when the month was over my stepfather said it was the best vacation he ever had. But it was sure an aggravating month for me." Tor emphasized his last statement by a slow serious nod of his head and slicing a thicker shaving from the gate.

"I'd already persuaded Grandpa that I ought to stay here and work and go to school from here. But Grandma Una was doubtful. Said she'd love having me for company, but being a woman she understood my mother's feeling about having me close to her.

"Every night I'd crawl out my window and listen on the porch roof to see if they were going to talk about it. Grandpa's rocker, seesawing up and down on the stone floor, used to drown out a few words, but I didn't miss much. Sometimes when it was still light enough for me to try to count chimney swallows diving down the chimneys, I'd miss a little—but not much.

"Mother used to say things like, 'He might grow away from us' or 'People might think he doesn't like his stepfather.'

"That was all bunk. Except sometimes when my stepfather called me Torrie. Then I hated him 'cause it sounded like a girl's name.

"Anyway, he'd say, 'The school is much better in the city.' And this didn't set too well with Grandpa. He'd stop his rocker and come right back and say, 'Our boys, Torm and Logan, went on to state college from the school at the foot of the mountain, and they both graduated high.' Grandpa was always leaning to my side.

"Then my stepfather would use a lot of big words like 'emotionally disturbed' and 'alienated affection' and 'split personality.' Grandpa would stop rocking and come back with, 'I've always thought most of these ailments come from too much pampering and spoiling, and a sure cure was a halter strap across the behind.'

"Grandpa gave it to me once. Remember, Shep, when he caught me and David Hillyer riding the calf after he'd told me it was too young and would be swaybacked the rest of its life if I rode it?

"But we won out, Shep. And Mother cried a little and walked around and around in the kitchen, saying, 'All right. We'll try it as long as he does well in school.' That's why I do my schoolwork and don't fight on the bus.

"When school first started, some kids used to say, 'Why do you stay on that lonesome mountain with them old people when you could live in the big city? Guess your new father don't want you.'

"That's why I know that people say mean things because they don't understand. The ones who say things like that don't know that Grandpa bought me four Cheviot ewes and a ram at the county fair, and said I owed him a hundred and twenty-seven dollars that I could pay back from wool and lambs when I built up my flock.

"We're set for life, Shep. One day I'll have a hundred sheep or more and all kinds of machinery to make work easy. Any year now, or maybe next, I'll start with a couple of young cattle. Grandpa will probably make me leave and go to state college like he did my pa. I hope not. But my stock will be growing all the time I'm gone."

Two gonglike rings of the farm bell that stood on a tall post by the kitchen door broke in on Tor's dreaming and whittling. The Bluetick hounds let out long whining bays because the bell's vibrations hurt their ears. It was Tor's signal from his grandma—two for Tor, one for mealtime, three for Grandpa, five for a visitor, and ten if the chimney caught fire. The bell would never again ring four times. Four, with long spaces, had been for Una MacLeod's own Torm; four without discernible spaces, for Logan.

Tor bounded from the gate with his knife still open—which Grandpa had told him never to do. He latched the gate as Grandpa had told him always to do.

"Let's go, Shep. Grandma says its chore time. Let's get some bread and jam or meat or somethin' first. God A'mighty! How that sun has dropped down."

❧ Three ❧

Tor and Shep came to the kitchen door together, Shep having to quicken his pace to a dogtrot once or twice to keep abreast of Tor's long strides. As they approached, Blue Boy and Tennessee Belle got up and walked to the edge of the stone step, wagging their tails. Shep measured each with a jealous eye as Tor lifted their long ears and let them run through his fingers as he passed. Tor liked the mellow buglelike bay of the hounds. He snapped his fingers just in front of the nose of each and said, "Bark!" Each hound let out two long winsome bays to the sky, then wagged their tails some more.

Tor gathered up his lunch box and book satchel. He scraped the mud from his boots on the scraper which had been made at the MacLeod forge by welding a heavy strip of iron between two horseshoes. Then he dragged his boots over the thick hemp mat which lay on the stone just before the door, saying to Shep as he did, "Wipe your feet, Shep." The dog responded by pulling one foot back and forth stiff-legged, after the manner of dogs when they meet a strange dog. Having performed the ritual, sacred to Grandma Una MacLeod and imposed by her on everyone, boy and dog disappeared behind the stockade-battened Dutch door that shivered with a metallic whimper on its long strap hinges and closed with a rattle and bang behind them.

"You must put some lard on those hinges, Angus," were the first words they heard from Grandma MacLeod when they were inside.

The mingled smell of cinnamon and apples made him instantly hungry. Without taking time to remove his coat, Tor dipped a brimming bowl of soup, heavy with meat and vegetables, from the black iron pot that sat on one of the back stove lids. From the warming closet above the pot he was able to snare three biscuits in one hand.

"Sure your eye isn't bigger than your stomach?" Angus MacLeod said as Tor seated himself next to his grandpa at the great oak table which divided the kitchen in its two halves—one for working, with its cookstove and cupboards; the other for living, with its fireplace, big enough for a boy to stand in, surrounded by a half circle of rocking chairs, all cushioned, seat and back. On one side of the fireplace a woodbox ran along the wall; on the other was a built-in cot which matched the age-darkened paneling of the wall.

"You forgot to wash your hands, and you sound like somebody playing a jew's-harp the way you eat your soup," Una MacLeod said with a half smile.

Angus MacLeod looked down at the boy and used up the other half of a smile. "He wants to show you how good your soup is, Mother." All MacLeod wives had been called Mother from the minute their first child was born.

Shep was alert to the sounds and scent of Tor's soup, too. He moved from his accustomed place on the hearth and stood by Tor's chair, wagging his tail. He might have been slipped a half of soft brown biscuit, except that Grandma MacLeod had a rule against it.

"Don't forget to change your jacket before you go to chores," Tor's grandma reminded him when she heard his spoon clanking at the bottom of the bowl.

"No lambs born today—I couldn't hear any from the barnyard gate," Tor said to his grandpa, having forgotten instantly what his grandma had said and not answering her.

"No, but as we been saying for a week—any day now. There're little spots of green showing where underground springs warm the land early, and more green showing all along the creek from the cold-spring field, so I let them run to graze today. A few sprigs of new grass are a real spring tonic; cleans out their systems and helps them bag up fast with plenty of milk when the lambs start dropping."

"Well, Shep and me had better be going to bring them in," Tor replied, pushing back his chair.

"Shep and I, please. I promised your mother I wouldn't let you fall in with school-bus talk," his grandmother said.

"No need to fetch the sheep." His grandpa put his hand on the boy's shoulder to steady him. "They'll be in at feeding time. They won't find that much new green. Besides, they can't roam too far. The mountain pasture gate has been closed since we brought them in before Christmas, when the first snow flurries started. How was school today?" This was a question that Angus MacLeod asked the boy often. He knew the answer before he asked, but the boy's grandmother puzzled over whether or not they were doing right by the child, and the answer comforted her.

"Good." This was the answer Angus MacLeod had expected. Now he waited for the slight variations that would make this school day different from any other.

Tor continued with sufficient enthusiasm to convince any doubter, "I finished my arithmetic first and Miss Haggerdy let me dust all the erasers and empty the pencil sharpener."

Of course Tor hated the smell of chalk dust and tablet paper and stale sawdust, but distinction carried its responsibility.

"I had more correct spelling words than Jim Rhodes, so the teacher let me move to a seat in front of him. I'm almost up to the front, and when I get there, I'll get another star on the spelling chart."

If Tor could have chosen a place to sit to learn, it would have been the top of a box stall in the barn, watching Grandpa teach a new calf to drink from a calf bucket; or in the hayloft door at the peak of the barn where he could look over the edge of the world and "take in half the county," as Grandpa said; or maybe atop a wooden gate, swinging in the breeze with his bootheels hooked behind the next to the top plank, where learning wasn't any different from dreaming.

"I read my reading lesson without missing a

word. When you do that you can go to the book-
shelf in the corner of the room and pick out a
storybook to read all by yourself. In my last year's
school you couldn't do that. There you had to
march in line on tiptoe into a big library, and
when you told the lady you wanted a horse or dog
story, she'd say, 'What kind of a horse story?' And
how was I to know whether she meant wild or
tame, or cowboy or plow horse? Then by that time
we'd have to line up to march back. There are five
horse books and three dog books at my school
now, and one book with all wild animals. I've seen
all the pictures more than ten times."

"I would say that was a good school day—
wouldn't you, Mother?"

"I would indeed," Una MacLeod replied and
smiled. "What do you want for that bread you've
got left, Tor, meat or jam?"

"Meat. But I'll get it." On the way around the
table Tor remembered another incident from his
school day that he considered worthy of note.
"Martha Hillyer said her father's farm was bigger
than ours. I said maybe so, but ours was the only
mountaintop farm. She said theirs was too, but I
said you couldn't call a farm that was just on the
side of the mountain a mountaintop farm. You
would call that a mountainside farm, I told her.
Then she said anyway they lived closer to Buena
Vista and went to a picture show every Saturday
afternoon. I said we'd never waste time going to
town except when we had to. Their farm is smaller
than ours, ain't it?"

"Isn't, not ain't, please, Tor," Una MacLeod interrupted. "I promised your mother I wouldn't let

you fall into that bad grammar you hear every day. And you shouldn't be sassy to Martha Hillyer. Her folks are our close and best neighbors, even though they do live three miles over the slope of the mountain."

"She said because their farm wasn't on the very top of the mountain"—and now Tor wished he hadn't started this statement, but he finished it, lowering his voice as he went—"her father said it would be spared if the highway was ever extended on from Thornton's Gap. Said her father had studied the land the government took for national forest and parkland and it was only a strip several miles wide along the very top of the mountain."

This time his grandfather didn't seem to hear the last remarks of Martha Hillyer, but said in a quiet, studied way, "Our farms are about the same size. His might be a little larger. It was two farms at one time. The land where the old deserted farmhouse stands used to be the McLean place. The original Hillyer house burned, and they bought the McLean place and lived there until a few years ago, when they built their new house. I still like the old McLean log house better than their new house. The old house is as sound as the day the first four chestnut logs were laid on the foundation."

"Our land is much flatter than theirs. Some of their fields are dangerous when it comes to using a tractor," Tor said, thinking he might lead Grandpa into a little tractor talk.

"But of course all our land except the fields up toward Hanging Gardens is much nearer being flat. David Hillyer is a good man. When he bor-

rows something, you never have to go get it."
Angus MacLeod began to pull on his boots, which
had been standing near the hearth. "It's about
chore time, I guess."

The man, the boy, and the dog went through
the door together; the boy with his biscuit, showing a large slab of reddish-brown ham which stuck
out on all sides of it. The half biscuit left over
from his soup had mysteriously disappeared. Outside the kitchen door he dropped two steps behind
his grandfather and slipped it from his pocket to
Shep. He also pulled off a narrow strip of meat
that wouldn't be needed to make his bread and
meat come out even, and gave it to the dog. Then
he caught up and lengthened his stride to keep
pace with the tall man. The boy was surrounded
by too many thoughts to remember that he hadn't
changed his good school Mackinaw.

The tall man measured the sun with his sharp
countryman's eye. He buttoned the top button of
his jacket. The sun had lost most of its early
March warmth. In another half hour it would disappear behind the Allegheny Mountains, far
across the valley in the west. The blue shadows of
rounded slope and ridge were already beginning
to dim. Angus MacLeod's high middle fields
would be the last to lose their luster. "Plenty of
time for all the chores with daylight left over," the
man said as he placed his hand on the boy's shoulder.

Four

Grandma MacLeod always signaled chore time for Tor long before the time required to do the work. She knew that a lot of figuring out and dreaming mixed in with work made the job longer but took the drudgery out of it.

So with the sun still a half hour high and more daylight now that it was March, Tor mixed work and play until he couldn't tell which was which because they both came out pure pleasure. A few steps alongside his grandpa and their paths parted. Grandpa went to the barn to milk and feed the big stock. Tor turned aside to the woodshed for kindling, stove wood, and fireplace logs. He had measured with his eye before he left the kitchen and knew that Grandma hadn't done any extra baking today. The cookstove woodbox was more than half full. The kindling basket always needed just one small armful of dry pine and the cobs from the corn sheller. The only thing he had to be particular about was to be sure and halve the small fireplace logs, or quarter the big ones, or Grandpa would complain. "No need to waste a whole log this time of year," Grandpa would say when he lit the fireplace at suppertime. "Just enough to take the chill off after the cookstove dies down."

Inside the woodshed Tor did the easiest job first. He split a dry pine stick into kindling pieces small enough so that he could break each one over his knee and make two. The grain of the wood curved around an amber-colored, resin-filled knot, shaped like a pine cone. He held the knot up close to his nose and smelled live pine needles. He could even smell the whole woodland and the damp swamp where the pine tree had grown. He studied the swirls and wavy designs before he laid the knot up on a beam, where he had a whole collection of pine knots. Grandpa called them candlewood and had pointed out the iron brackets on the stone face of the chimney above the mantel where they'd been used to light the house and save candles before coal oil—even before Grandpa.

About two armfuls of stove sticks would fill the box to the brim. Tor estimated one armful of hemlock and sassafras and one of oak and beech. Grandma liked soft hemlock and sassafras for a quick fire but hard oak and beech to keep it steady for even cooking. Grandpa liked the smell of sassafras in the cookstove and applewood in the fireplace.

Grandpa ranked the applewood in a separate pile and used it in the dead of winter when more of the day was spent in front of the fire. So Tor slabbed off a few fireplace pieces from a triangle of an oak log that Grandpa had quartered with his wedge and maul. Before he began the job of carrying in, he counted the growth rings on one of the quarter pieces that was left. As near as he could make out, the tree had lived ninety-six years. Some rings were wide and some were narrow. "Wet years and dry years," Tor said to himself. His grandpa had explained all this before. Tor also knew that the tree had grown over a ledge, with one side of its roots in rock crevices and sparse ground and the other side in good earth. The rings on the rock side were all much smaller. "That's why the tree was lopsided and not a true circle." Grandpa had pointed this out, too.

When Tor had carried in the wood by the armful, because the wood cart was too hard to push in the spring mud, his next stop was the corncrib. On the side of the corn sheller opposite the crank there was a heavy balance wheel whose weight kept the sheller going for a dozen ears or more, once there was enough momentum. Tor swung his weight from side to side as the crank moved around and around. It took two hands to start the machine with its clank-clank. But as it speeded up and whirled with a rhythmic clackety-clack-clack, one hand was enough. When it got fast enough to almost lift Tor off the floor, he let go of the crank and fed the golden ears into the hopper, where sharp iron fingers grabbed one ear at a time and pushed it between the two burred shelling discs. The grains poured into a tin bucket from one spout, the cobs into a basket from another.

Some cobs came out white, some pink. Tor made a game of trying to guess which would come next. Now and then, if an especially smooth cob hit the basket, Tor would lay it aside to make a bubble pipe or something.

There was scarcely an end to what a boy could do with a good smooth cob if he had a pocketknife with a gimlet. Once after Grandpa had pointed out a woody-stemmed plant with narrow grayish leaves called rabbit tobacco that grew in the pasture and had said the Indians used to smoke it when their tobacco crop was short, Tor had made a real corncob pipe with an elderberry stem and got sick as a dog smoking rabbit tobacco behind the stone wall when he went for the cows. When he brought the cows late and didn't want any supper, his grandmother had said he looked awful peaked and made him go to bed early.

Before Tor left the corncrib, he counted the rows of kernels on several ears. Grandpa had offered him a dollar bill if he ever found an ear that had an odd number of rows. "They're always even," Grandpa said. "Nature never changes her pattern. Just like she always puts five needles in a bunch on a white pine." Tor had counted a lot of pine needles, too, and found that his grandpa was right.

Tor gave some shelled corn to the chickens and took the rest to the barn for Grandpa to feed a couple of aged workhorses. Their teeth were no longer strong enough to eat it off the cob. But Grandpa said, "They've earned their rest, and a horse of mine will never go to the soap factory to be butchered." At the barn he left the corn on the barn floor. Grandpa liked to feed the old horses himself and rub his hand over the head of each.

As Tor climbed the ladder to the hayloft, he heard his grandfather talking to the cows at the far end of the barn, calling them by name as each stanchion closed with a clank. He heard the sheep bells in the distance and listened long enough, halfway up the ladder, to know that the sheep were slowly coming in. Shep sat on the barn floor looking up.

The woodshed and corncrib were fun. But there was nothing to equal the barn. Here all the powers of sight, sound, and smell were not enough to capture what was real and what was mystery.

Through knotholes, louvers, and cracks above sagging doors, shafts of sunlight shot like giant arrows through barn dust. And beyond the shafts of light there were eerie corners, dimming into darkness, where hay chaff caught in cobwebs hung like witches' veils. Sounds of the stomp of hoof and neigh of horse, the rattle of stanchion and bellow of hungry calf, the bleat of sheep and music from their bells, all became faraway and mysterious when heard from the barn loft.

There were other sounds, too. Sounds of a mother cat calling her kittens to safety under the barn floor, and the muffled meow of some stray tomcat from behind stacks of hay bales, his yellow eyes shining out from a narrow slit between wall and hay, not sure he would be welcomed and given a pan of warm milk, or be put upon by someone yelling "Scat," and a sharp-pronged pitchfork cutting the air too close behind him. Sounds of loft boards forever swelling and contracting on giant beams, responding with muted creaks against each other's pegged joints to a breeze rising outside. Pigeons cooing in rafters and cupola. And drifting down from above the cupola the slow or rapid whine of the running-horse weather vane telling the wind's story.

It took time to gather in the smells of the barn. There were always smells that brought the fields and seasons inside and softened them. The rancid aroma of manure which bespoke tall corn for harvesttime, when it was spread and turned to earth under deep furrows. The musty smell of knee-deep chaff and the oat bin where a mouse, moving however carefully, could start an avalanche and bring a cat on tiptoe. The dainty whiff of golden straw, with stems to chew on and conjure up a picture of undulating waves of a thousand spears of sunshine on a grainfield racing from fence to fence. Smells of horse dandruff, stale sweat and leather mixed in harness, cows' garlic breath in spring, and wool grease in downy fleeces. And sifting from the hayloft through all other smells and dominating them, the fragrance of green fields in June and honey-laden bloom of clover.

Here, too, were lessons for the heart of a boy. An aged horse, its freedom from plow and wagon earned, standing on stiffening joints, with trot and proud prance forever gone, teaching that nothing outgallops time. A newborn calf or lamb, bracing its rubbery legs to reach life-giving milk, picturing the urgency of life to grow strong—to make ready to race an April breeze the full circle of a field or play leapfrog with a brook or pasture ditch.

From the top of the loft ladder Tor spoke gently to Shep. "Move, Shep. I don't want to let you have it with a bale of hay. I've tried it a couple of times with an ornery cat when Grandpa said, 'They're too many cats in this barn,' but I always missed because they were too fast for me. They sure scatted, though, when they saw that bale headed down through the air."

The boy strained his eyes to see into the dark corners. The flutter of a wing in the rafters and the plaintive cooing from the cupola above added enough mystery to the dimness to send a chill up his spine as he moved quickly to open the loft door.

He turned the bales end over end and watched them somersault through the loft hole to the floor below, counting the right number for the inside stock. Then he watched the right number for the outside racks and sheep shed catapult from the loft door and bounce on the ground below. He studied the long rope which hung from the peak of the roof. He would save it for another day—to carry it to the highest beam, then swing above the hay, trying to touch the rafters. Besides, it was more fun to swing when the hay was almost gone and it was a long way down to the floor of the loft.

By the time Tor closed the loft door and reached the ladder hole he could almost see strange eyes glaring at him from the dark corners of the barn. Below him Angus MacLeod was about to carry the last bale of hay to its proper manger. Tor called down to him, "How many runaway slaves did your pa find hiding in the hayloft?"

Tor had heard the stories of runaway slaves and Half-faced John before, but they always gave him the shivers. He liked the way Grandpa described the scared eyes of the slaves and the one eye of Half-faced John.

"Oh, lots of them," Angus MacLeod replied as he put down the bale he had just picked up and seated himself on it.

"There were never as many slaves in this part of the state," Angus began. This was the part that Tor didn't find too exciting, but it was where Grandpa always started.

The boy sat down beside the man and found a hay stem to chew on until the history part of the story was finished.

"One reason for that was the land wasn't suited for cotton and tobacco growing. Another reason was that this part of the state was settled mainly by people who had started in the North where slavery never caught on much. Most of them were of Scotch and Irish descent. They had fought for their own freedom against the King of England, and they knew what freedom meant. Most of them and their forebears had been poor and never expected much from life except to be independent and to be able, without bowing down to any man, to put enough bread on the table. Over in the tidewater part of the state and farther south, there was more of a yearning to grab the land and get rich quick by working both land and slaves to death.

"Our folks would never have slaves. My father said it was because MacLeods tried to live by the golden rule. I reckon he was right. But to tell you the truth, mountain farms were mostly stock farms. That is, there was more land in pasture than for crops. So slaves weren't needed much. But there were some slaves in the valley.

"The big stir started in the late fall of 1859, as my father told me."

Tor stirred and turned himself so he could watch his grandpa's eyes. At last he was coming to the exciting part of the story.

"Well, there had always been a dribble of runaways. And when they ran away, they took to the mountain to move north with the ridges. So every once in a while Pa would come out in the morning and find one hiding in the hayloft, nearly starved and scared half to death, maybe hoping to steal a chicken or something. Sometimes already two or three empty corncobs in the hay beside him from eating hard raw corn. That was better than acorns which they lived on in the woods.

"It was a pitiful sight the way Pa remembered it. The runaways would crawl out of the corner on their hands and knees, like a cowed stray dog at a kitchen door. They'd plead, 'Marse, we ain't meant no harm. We've been whupped to death. All we need is a few vittles to help us on.' Pa would take them to the house and feed and warm them. Sometimes they'd eat a dozen biscuits with meat and gravy. Then with a poke of biscuits my mother would bake while they were eating, and a few slabs of meat if it could be spared, they'd go out the kitchen door praying and blessing the 'missus.' If they made it along the ridges to the Potomac and got across, they stood a chance of getting to the Quaker land of Pennsylvania and freedom. But the Potomac was hard to pass.

"Slave hunters rode both sides. They were a

hard lot, making a living by capturing runaways and returning them for reward, or more often stealing them to sell for their own profit to a trader.

"Pa said even a starving slave would never steal like a slave hunter. Said they usually rode in threes or fours. Said they'd ride up to a farmhouse after dark, and while one was asking questions at the kitchen door, the others would be stealing a ham or two from the smokehouse; smokehouses always being pretty far from the house because of fire danger.

"They didn't show up here much, with their guns resting across the pommels of their saddles and long whips hanging by their sides, until the fall of '59, when there was a whole rash of runaways from the valley."

Tor wanted Grandpa to get to more slaves in the hayloft. But he had long since learned from a stern look around the fireplace, and Grandma Una saying, "Don't interrupt your grandfather," that Grandpa would tell the story his own way.

"In the fall of '59 word spread up and down the valley like wildfire, from cabin to cabin, that there was a man at Harper's Ferry named John Brown who had an army, and wagons hauling runaways day and night to Chambersburg, Pennsylvania, where a man named Shields Green, who'd been a slave himself, waited with other wagons to haul slaves to freedom.

"There was no truth to the story, but they wanted to believe it so much they reckoned it had to be true. Late in November, when John Brown and Shields Green were in the Charles Town jail, sentenced to be hanged, runaways still believed the first story, and still kept trying to make it to Harper's Ferry.

"Whole families tried to make it along the mountain, all headed for Harper's Ferry, where they'd ride the rest of the way to freedom. There got to be so many runaways that owners took their slaves' shoes away at night or put padlocks on cabin doors and locked them in.

"My pa and mother fed a lot of them. Didn't try to change their story, but let them go on. The story my mother always used to tell was the saddest of all.

"Two days after Thanksgiving that year there was a snow squall in the night. Enough only to salt and pepper the ground but make the stones completely white. When Pa came to the barn that morning, he found barefoot tracks on the stones just outside the feed-room door. He could tell by the tracks that there was more than one. He opened the door and said, 'Come outa there!' But there wasn't a sound. So he took a corn knife in his hand and climbed the ladder to the loft.

"There they were, cowering in the corner, their eyes as big as the bottom of a teacup when they saw him with that corn knife.

"When Pa saw that it was a man and woman with a child in her arms, he dropped the corn knife down the ladder hole and said, 'Come on out.'

"Well, it was a pitiful sight. The child was dead. A little girl four or five years old. The man saying, 'We'll go, Marse. We ain't meant no harm.' And the woman just holding the child in her arms. Not making a whimper.

"The man followed Pa down the ladder. When his head was even with the loft door, the woman bent over and gave him the child in one arm. Pa tried to get him to hand it down to him, but the man held onto the child and came down grasping the rungs of the ladder with one hand.

"They were so scared and hopeless that they started out the door without even asking for food and warmth. Pa calmed their fears and got them started toward the kitchen. He went ahead to warn your great-grandmother. He knew she'd be mighty broken up. She and your great-grandpa were both still young. Only your great-uncle Mohr had been born then.

"While your great-grandmother put them by the fire and fed them, Pa laid out the child in the front room, wrapped in a white coverlet. When they'd finished eating, Pa took them in to see the child. The woman said, 'Now she's done got warm too.' And they were the only words she spoke the whole day. They put her to bed by the fire. But all day long she'd get up and go in the front room and stand over the child. My mother would have to lead her back and tuck the covers around her.

"Pa and the young man talked, though. They'd left the flatland somewhere on the upper James River, before it goes through the mountains toward Lynchburg. They'd been two days and nights on the ridges, headed for Harper's Ferry. Somebody had told them they could make it in a week, and that the woods were full of acorns and there were lots of mountain farms with plenty of ear corn still standing in the shock.

"The child got wheezy the first night. The second day it was croupish. The man and woman took turns carrying it all that day. When they got to Pa's barn late the second night, they held it over the manger so it could breathe a horse's warm breath. That loosened up its lungs just like the steam kettle on the kitchen stove does. Then they climbed into the loft to rest until daylight. The child was asleep and breathing easy. It just didn't wake up. Not a whimper, died in its sleep."

"Why was that, if it was better?" Tor interrupted without taking his eyes off the darkness above the loft hole. For the sun was gone.

"The warm breath of the horse was mostly carbon dioxide. So it was really doing more harm than good.

"But to finish the story. There was some excitement that day. Pa was in the shed making a coffin to bury the child. Three slave hunters rode up and asked if he'd seen a man and woman with a child. My mother had heard the hooves and taken the man and woman to the attic. Grandpa Ennis MacLeod, your great-great-grandpa, he was still alive then, sat at the kitchen window with his muzzleloader. Said he'd drop the first one on the doorstep if they tried to come in the house. But when the slave hunters saw Pa was making a coffin, and he told them his child had died with the croup, they rode away.

"Pa dug a grave right there in the graveyard. Grandpa Ennis said to dig it right beside Flora's grave. Flora MacLeod was your great-great-grandmother. They started to bury it after chores, but the woman stood over it and said, 'Let it stay in the warm one more night.'

"So they buried it the next morning. My mother gave the man Pa's Sunday shoes and the woman hers. She loaded them with all the vittles she could spare, and they disappeared north along the ridge."

"Why'd they let them go?" Tor asked in a wavering voice. "It was still ninety miles to Harper's Ferry and nothing there when they got there."

"I guess they talked about it. Grandpa said they had one chance in a hundred since the weather had moderated. Said it 'was the devil on one side and a rock pile on the other.' So what could they do? Besides, the law was awful strict about harboring a runaway.

"After the war was over, and black people were free to go wherever they wanted, my mother used to think they might come back to see where their child was buried. When they never did, she thought they hadn't made it across the Potomac.

"It's still in the graveyard chart that's in the big Bible. Right between Flora and Ennis MacLeod, in Grandpa's script. He marked it 'God's Child.'

"Now let's put the rest of the hay in the racks. You've heard about Half-faced John and all the other stories a dozen times."

Tor was glad he didn't have to go back up to the hayloft. The sheep bells tinkled as the sheep pushed each other around the feed trough. Tor counted his white-faced Cheviots among his grandpa's many Highlands. They had all come in, and there were no lambs.

Angus MacLeod ran his eye over his Highlands. "Those three ewes standing apart and not wanting feed will drop theirs tonight, I guess," he said as he pushed the wooden bolt of the door into its worn socket.

The blue shadows were already climbing up over the fields that lay to the east. In the little daylight that was left over, the man and boy walked toward the house. Shep, who had grown restless sitting too long on the barn floor, danced in and out between them.

❧ Five ❧

None of the red blood of Scotch Highlanders had been leached out by the generations which separated Angus MacLeod from his sturdy forebears who had crossed the sea, penetrated the wilderness, and tamed it. That same blood surged through Angus MacLeod's veins. He was a mountain man. He loved his mountain farm. He moved unruffled with the path of the sun, seldom missing its first beams striking the top of the Hanging Gardens and its last light on the stone walls at the edge of the farthest western fields. He worked six days a week and rested the seventh.

In winter after chores and supper he read the daily paper that the mailman brought a day late from the county seat. In summer the ritual changed. After the long day in the fields he rocked on the porch through the twilight and asked Una MacLeod if there was any news. Sometimes what he heard started him talking about how times were changing. But he tried to keep his own world with as little change as possible, the one thing about the man which the boy Tor hoped to change.

He went to the Presbyterian church on Sundays. He entered his Black-faced Highland sheep and his yearling Shorthorn bulls at the county fair. Once a year Una MacLeod badgered him into going to the Farm Bureau picnic. He went to the church picnic without being badgered. He went to the courthouse to vote and to serve on the jury when he was called.

He provided for the wants of his family, which was not difficult. MacLeod pride reached its highest expression in the self-sufficiency and secure warmth that came from what could be grown and made, not in what could be had for a price.

"I hate Martha Hillyer and those girls on the bus," Tor said at the supper table. The appreciation which had been expressed by Grandpa and his grandmother earlier for Martha Hillyer's parents hadn't settled the matter in Tor's mind.

"Is that grit still grinding in your craw?" Angus MacLeod asked with a smile which quickly changed to a frown when he noticed that Tor had helped himself to about half the crust from the steaming shepherd's pie and almost none of the vegetables and mutton under the crust.

"Well, there're other things, too," Tor continued. "She's always throwing up about how I caught the sleeve of her party dress in the cogwheel of the grindstone at the birthday party Mother and Grandmother had for me last summer. Says it was frayed and ripped all the way to the elbow, and her mother had to make a short-sleeved dress out of it. I was against it all the time. Told Mother birthday parties were for town kids who didn't have anything else to do. But she wouldn't hear to it. I hope I never have to have another one."

"I think Martha Hillyer would look just as pretty in a short-sleeved party dress as a long-sleeved one." Tor's grandmother smiled across the table to Angus. Her remark also provided Tor with time to chew the mouth-wide slab of golden-brown shepherd's pie crust he had just balanced skillfully on his fork.

When he spoke again, it was not to agree or disagree with his grandmother's observation. He had further evidence as to the evils attending and following unwanted birthday parties in the country.

"You said yourself, Grandpa, that it was a lot of tomfoolery. When the boys were trying to run away from the girls and left all the gates open, and the beef steers got mixed up with the cows, and Dan McAlpin was afraid of the cows and fell in the watering trough running backward."

"Maybe I meant leaving gates open was a lot of tomfoolery."

"But you said when you were a boy and it was your birthday, your pa would bend you over his knee and give you as many gentle swats as you were old, and one hard one to grow on. Said when you were about my age, he gave you your choice of two pigs, two lambs, or a calf, and said fatten and market them, buy twice the number of small ones, and put the leftover money in the bank."

"Well, I guess that's about the way it was. But about hating these girls. When I was a boy that was about the same as it is now. We didn't have much chance to hate them at the district school. There wasn't a school bus. Each family's children went by themselves, walking or on horseback or in a buggy, depending on how far and how many. At school the boys sat on one side of the room and the girls on the other. At recess boys played on one side of the school lot, the girls on the other.

"The only convenient place we had for hating girls was at church. There boys and girls were mixed in the same Sunday school class until they finished the Shorter Catechism. The boys always tried to all get in the back seat, but sometimes there wasn't room and a boy would have to slide in on the end of the girls' row. That happened to me several times, and I always ended up by a girl who was the preacher's daughter. She always got to answer the question that I missed so I whispered 'Smarty' and hated her. Her name was Una Logan."

Tor looked across at his grandmother with a sheepish grin.

"Then when I was about fourteen, at a church picnic, I walked through the graveyard with her after we had eaten. She had ribbons on the ends of her long braids, and I thought she was awful pretty. I was snapping twigs off the boxwoods and mock oranges as we walked, and she said I oughtn't to. Then I tried to snap a blade off a sword lily and got a bad cut on my finger. She looked at it and held my hand to see better and said, 'That's what you get for being destructive to the dead.' All the way back to the church I was sucking the blood out, so we didn't talk any. But I was remembering that she had held my cut hand for a minute and had let it go very gently.

"We weren't in the same class anymore, but I saw her every Sunday across the church. Before long, two or three years, I guess, I was going to church twice on Sunday. Driving Pa's buggy down to evening devotional and taking Una Logan home.

"But that ended. She went thirty miles away to normal school for two years to become a teacher. Too far to go to visit. Those were mighty long years. She only got home at Christmas and Easter.

"She always had a mind of her own, and I couldn't change it. Said she owed it to her parents to teach two years and use her education because they had made a sacrifice to help her get it. So she did. Then her father married us outside under the trees in the churchyard after the church picnic. She said I picked that day because I didn't want to lose a half day's work some other time.

"You see. That's what happens to girl haters. That's how your grandmother came to be."

Supper was over. Angus MacLeod moved to his place by the hearth. Una MacLeod didn't want him to get on the subject of the boys, Torm and Logan, and how after Logan was born, the doctor had said she couldn't have the four more children she wanted to make an average MacLeod family. So she gave the boy an understanding smile and changed the subject: "Tell Tor about the stranger we had today."

Tor put his plate on the drainboard and moved to a chair next to his grandfather until time to dry the dishes for his grandmother. He hoped the stranger had been a salesman who'd sold Grandpa a big red tractor. Martha Hillyer was still running through his head. Could Grandpa be right about what happened to girl haters? When Martha Hillyer wasn't talking, she could be right pretty. He was sorry he'd brought up the name of Martha Hillyer. He'd sure remember never to mention her again. He knew lots of kids his age who said they drove their fathers' tractors. Martha Hillyer said her brother drove a tractor when he was eight. Said her father referred to Grandpa's way of farming as old-fashioned. But he'd never tell Grandpa that. It would either make him angry or hurt his feelings.

"Was he sellin' or beggin'?" Tor asked, using an expression his grandpa always said to himself whenever a shiny big car stopped at the mailbox and a man got out wearing Sunday clothes in the middle of the week.

"Beggin'," Angus MacLeod replied. "A man from over the mountain at Fredericksburg, beggin' to buy the two big boxwood plants that stand outside the MacLeod graveyard. Offered me a hundred dollars apiece, and they'd send men to dig them. Seems they're getting ready for some big historical celebration and want to put James Monroe's law office building back the way it was when he practiced law there.

"I told him it wouldn't be showing much respect for the MacLeod sleeping under the sod inside who'd set them out a hundred years or more ago. I told him that all this fad of buying up old relics and restoring things had started with the Rockefellers spending all that money in Williamsburg.

"Why, I can remember when an iron kettle or coffee grinder wouldn't bring a quarter at an auction.

"He was a nice enough man. But I told him if

people took care of things, they wouldn't have to be restored.

"He said the two white cedars that stand inside the graveyard gate were the largest he's ever seen except the ones along Cedar Creek under Natural Bridge. He called them by another name—arborvitum or arborvitae I think he said. I showed him the date 1823 chiseled in the bottom stone of the gate column, and he said he thought the boxwoods and the cedars were as old as the column."

Tor's dream of the big red tractor was gone for the moment. He was thinking he'd take a closer look at the trees in the graveyard. They might be higher to climb than the ones in the apple orchard, if the needles weren't prickly like fencepost cedars.

Indeed the MacLeod graveyard prompted sufficient interest to stop an occasional stranger just passing through on the mountain road. Except for lacking a wide gate and catwalk, it might readily have been mistaken for a stone stockade. It was easily an acre in size, laid out in a perfect square. The head-high walls were wide enough and sufficiently smooth for a boy to run along the top without fear of falling. The massive stones had been shaped and so carefully joined that it is doubtful whether or not a chipmunk could have found a joint wide enough to offer refuge from a hungry cat. There was no mortar binding stone to stone, but not a single stone had moved in the nearly one hundred and fifty years since the last one had been put in place. Some MacLeod, proud of his share in the work, had chiseled "1823" deep in the bottom stone by the gate.

Clumps of lilacs ran along the wall which faced the orchard. A spiked iron gate, hammered into shape at the MacLeod forge, still standing across the road from the house, led through the wall. Inside the wall there were no gravestones. A chart in an ancient Bible, kept on the parlor table, marked the resting place of each MacLeod, along with date of birth and death.

In summer Angus MacLeod separated out a half dozen gentle sheep to keep the plot clipped. Each Decoration Day some ladies drove up from an organization in the town and stuck flags on the graves of Angus MacLeod's brother Ross and his and Una's boys, Torm and Logan. Angus always took the sheep out the day before they came. He also drove a stake at the head of each grave so the ladies could find where to put the flags. He considered the whole thing a waste of time. But Una said the town people might think it disrespectful to have animals grazing over the dead.

"There's not a MacLeod out there who wouldn't prefer the bleat of a Black-faced Highland to the rattle of a mowing machine," Angus would say.

Una MacLeod would smile understandingly. There was little in Angus MacLeod's world or Angus MacLeod that she ever would have considered changing very much, even if she had thought change possible.

"When the man from Fredericksburg saw the watering trough, he wanted to buy it," Angus MacLeod continued before Tor could ask if white cedars had prickly needles. "Said he'd seen them hollowed out of half a log, but never one out of a solid block of limestone that would hold twice as much water as a bathtub. He looked for a date on it. I told him that by the time it was finished there probably wasn't enough left of strength in man or iron in the chisel to even score the numbers.

"He said these people, meaning us, sure built things not to wear out. That he guessed the one thing that ever wore out was the people themselves.

"I told him mountain men didn't wear out; that they were like oak trees—either had to be chopped down or blown over."

"What in the world would the town of Fredericksburg do with a watering trough in this age?" Una MacLeod asked.

"He said it would be perfect to go alongside of a big round sandstone block at the corner of one of the streets where slaves used to be auctioned off. Said one side had steps hewn in it where people used to mount their horses.

"The next thing he wanted to buy was all the windows out of the house. Said there'd be enough for both James Monroe's law office and the John Paul Jones' house, where Jones lived from 1768 to 1775. Offered to send men to take them out, put in new ones and clean up after. Wanted me to name a price."

"You should've done it, Grandpa," Tor interrupted. "They're hard to see out of. Some of them make everything ripply, and others have whirlpools in the glass."

"I told him seven generations of MacLeods had looked out of them at sheep and cattle grazing mountain pastures. They'd watched the seasons change and looked for good signs and bad in movement of the clouds, so we'd have to keep them. That new windows would rob us of things we liked to remember."

"He must have been really put out with you, Grandpa. Not selling him anything he wanted."

"No. He was real understanding. Said even if we didn't do any business, he was glad he'd come over; that he'd like to come back and bring his children. I told him to come anytime, and welcome."

Una MacLeod had cleared the table. "It's schoolwork time, Tor," she said.

The boy put his book satchel on the table. Took a long time sharpening his pencil at the fireplace, then went about his work. Shep moved from the hearth and stretched out at the boy's feet under the table.

❧ Six ❧

The MacLeod house was like nothing else in the county, and quite likely the state also. In summer it mellowed with the life and warmth of the earth and looked as though it might have been a wagon hostel on an ancient turnpike, a welcome sight to weary travelers.

Except for barns and sheds on the north side that were lined with it against the sky, the orchard which ran west from the unfenced dooryard, and a giant maple stump holding only half a tree, all was open. Foundation planting was not for mountain men. "No shrubs and trees to hamper a man's vision" was the way they put it. In winter this starkness gave the house the appearance of a fortress.

The structure of the house itself made it distinctive among houses. It was built of logs. The kitchen wing, which had been the original house, with its steep roof and rafter loft for sleeping, was of logs hewn on two sides and chinked with lime mortar.

Angus MacLeod's great-grandfather had built the two-story addition, which was the main house, to house his thirteen children. The logs of the main house had been hewn on all four sides. Each log was more than a foot square, twice the size of average building logs. Instead of the half notch to join the corners, they were dovetailed after the manner of a cabinetmaker joining parts of fine furniture.

Except at close inspection, the sides looked as though they were an unbroken wall of wood. Close observation revealed that the cracks between logs, none scarcely more than half an inch, had been packed with grease wool from MacLeod sheep. The wool with its natural oils provided insulation against cold and dampness. Treated with lye, leached from wood ashes, the wool packing also insured against mice and insects. Angus Mac-Leod was proud of the fact that it had taken science a hundred years to "come up with an insulation that equaled it."

A wide porch ran the whole length of the main house. The lawn before the front door showed no path; but one, well worn and indented in the earth, led to the kitchen door.

A massive chimney of uncut fieldstone stood at the end of the kitchen wing. Another halved the peak of the main house's mottled red-and-gray slate roof. The kitchen roof was of wood shingles; some curled up to the sun with age, others grew moss on their damp ends.

Out from this center MacLeod fields ran in all directions. Save on the north side, where they slanted sharply upward toward the woodland and the naked cliffs of the Hanging Gardens, their roll was gentle. Their farthest edges ended at the skyline.

Eons far back of measured time had helped the

smoothing off and leveling with wind, rain, frost—
the heavings and settlings in the bosom of the
earth. For MacLeod's mountain was part of the
Appalachians, the oldest mountains on earth except for the Urals.

But nature's work aside, what Angus MacLeod
saw when he looked out of his windows, or stood
leaning against a porch post, was chiefly what he
and other MacLeods had coaxed forth, rear-
ranged, and brought into being, fragment by fragment, from a wilderness.

The ax had pushed back the forest. The seeder's
swinging hand and measured step had persuaded
the green life to the outermost edge of the land.
Stumps had been chopped at and burned until
they had disappeared from the earth. Stone sleds
pulled by oxen, moving no faster than the upland
clouds against which they were silhouetted—before planting in spring and after harvest in autumn
—had made their endless trips back and forth
until the land was clean.

The stones had been placed one upon the other
to bind and hold each against frost and heave until
they were shoulder high. Finished with the flattest
ones saved for the top. They followed swale and
rise, fencing in and fencing out. They gave pattern
to the land and design and character to fields.
Here and there stones had also been used to ter-
race a ravine to hold back spring's unfrozen
streams and summer's thunderheads from eroding
the earth.

There were other patterns on the land of Angus
MacLeod. The zigzag stitch of ancient rail fences
held some fields together. Only those made of

chestnut remained. Gray and weathered, they would defy time. Left at irregular intervals, grown tall and straight, red cedar and locust stood for old fences to lean on. Deep grooves of wagon roads and paths made by sheep and cattle, walking in single file, wound from gate to gate, circling a swale or halving the rim of a knoll.

This was the world which Tor entered when he left the school bus day after day. It was the only world of Angus MacLeod. It was a world where Angus MacLeod paced his life to the rise and fall of the sun. A world where young Tor MacLeod quickened his pace to keep astride the sure-cadenced step of the tall mountain man, lest he miss the pulsebeat of the earth, vibrating from the man's footfalls.

The boy was Angus MacLeod's only remaining blood. He knew that it was natural for a boy to respond to the earth. But he also knew that the world was changing, that men were souring on the land and leaving it. He must put the land in the blood of the boy. He must plant there the faith that the earth would remain, with its seedtime and harvest, that the sun would return after the storm and bridge the mountain with a rainbow.

So in spring when the man and the boy went to the orchard to plant a tree to fill a space left by one grown old and toppled by the wind, the boy would say, "There're plenty of trees left."

And the man would answer, "A gap in the row is unsightly."

The boy would say, "But it takes so long before it grows and bears."

The man would answer, "Maybe not in my time

but in yours. If somebody hadn't kept the gaps filled long ago, all the orchard would be gone."

Then the boy understood and copied the man, pressing the soft earth down upon the roots with his boot to make the sapling stand firm and hold its few thin boughs up to the sun.

In summer the lesson of the land was everywhere. Resting in the shade at the end of a long corn row, with corn high enough for its greenblack blades to kiss a boy's cheeks as he passed, the man would fill his hand with earth and let it sift through his fingers, saying as he did, "This used to be all forest. After the trees were cut to fill the woodshed or build a barn or shed, the stumps and stones were left. It was called newground. Turning newground into a field took time. The plow would hook on roots or stones and snap the beam. Harness and singletrees would break, and horses' shoulders would get galled. Sprouts would grow back and try to choke out the seeds. But each year a few more stumps would give way. Stones pushed up by frost were hauled off between plowing time and seeding and laid on the walls. Then one winter, a man sitting by the fireplace, dreaming of spring with his boots off and his heavy wool socks too close to the fire and beginning to singe, would say, 'There're only three stumps left in the newground. It'll be a good field by the end of plowing this year.' That would be eight or nine years from the start. Maybe ten."

The man, finishing his story, would see the boy filling his small hand with earth and letting it trickle through his fingers.

Angus MacLeod had passed this way before. He

had known the fields in their seasons as a boy with his father. He had shown his sons, Torm and Logan, how the earth could be coaxed to respond. Passing from generation to generation, these lessons were too precious for even one to be lost.

So another day Angus MacLeod stopped turning the mountainous windrows of new-mown hay up to the sun and walked with the boy to the edge of the field, where a spring gurgled from under the wall that separated hayfield and pasture. He drank from a rusty tin cup left on the wall from another year, then passed a cupful to the boy, saying as he did, "This is an artificial spring. You see where all those little swales run one after the other halfway across the field where the windrows dip? Well, my pa said when he was a boy they were all filled with water half the year from underground springs.

"It aggravated my grandpa that it stayed too wet to plow, and nothing grew except pussy willows, red dogwood, and Indian bromegrass. So one summer when the crops were laid by, he plowed a ditch as deep as he could plow it across the field. Then he plowed other ditches and joined all the wet spots to the main ditch. Then year after year he dug the ditches deeper. That was before tractors and power shovels, but he wouldn't have used one anyway.

"When the ditches were deep enough, he hauled stones and laid up conduits, bottom, sides and top, with flat stones. Deep enough that a plow could pass above them. Where he found flat stones enough, I'll never know. Then he shoveled and plowed back earth to cover them, a foot deep or more. That's how he made a marsh into a field.

"You can hear the water running underground. Come, I'll show you."

The man and boy straddled a dozen windrows, kicking the dry hay as they walked. The boy knelt by the man and put his ear against the earth. Far below he heard the muffled gurgle of water over stone.

"Hear it?" the man asked.

The boy listened for a long time. "Will it ever fall in?" he said at last.

"Never. Unless there's an earthquake," the man replied.

The lesson of autumn which Tor MacLeod soaked up from following his grandpa was the lesson of fulfillment and contentment. Man and earth had done their work. The boy watched the man draw a mark on the potato bin at the level to which it had been filled, put the number of the year by the mark, and say, "Plenty." For the corn-crib and the oat bin he would do the same above or below other marks and years, pointing to one low on the plank and saying, "This was a dry year, or this was the year of the big hailstorm."

In autumn, too, the man would show the boy the fields at rest. "I think old Blue Boy and Tennessee Belle would like to start a fox. The moon is right," he would say. So man and boy would cross the fields up to the woodland by the Hanging Gardens, stand and look back upon the land, mottled gray and gold by the hunter's full moon. Then find a spot to sit and listen to the music of the chase.

And when the moon was up the sky, far past a boy's bedtime, and a wise fox had tired of sporting with the hounds and was safe in his den behind some ledge, man and boy would cross the fields again. Home to a mug of warm cider from the back lid of the stove, with cinnamon sprinkled on the suds.

Winter was the time for a man's heart to warm with care for his own barn critters and with respect for God's ways with his wild ones. It was the time to lure meadowlarks to the barn lot with scattered grain and save their song for summer fields; time to honor the claim of a field mouse where its cornsilk igloo was built in the corner of a barn shelf; time to move softly near the barn eaves where a screech owl blinked at the low sun and sheltered himself from the wind.

"Winter's quiet renews a man's faith; faith that makes him impatient for the seasons to finish their circuit and hurry to planting time," Angus MacLeod said to Tor as they stood far out in the snow-covered fields, on a cold late January day. The quiet was broken only by the tapping of a woodpecker on a hollow fence post. The rat-tat-tat bounced against a wall across the field and drifted back over the snow as an echo.

Tor shifted his weight from boot to boot. His feet were cold, his fingers numbing in spite of gloves and pockets. The sun's last thin rind had dropped behind the mountains, and instantly the boy was colder. All the fields looked alike. He wondered why his grandfather turned this way and that, then turned and looked some more. He wanted to say, "Let's go," but still he didn't.

"My pa used to say a man should walk all his fields at least once in winter. Said that in the other seasons a man would be partial to this one or that, depending on the crop or what was grazing. But if he came to them in winter, he'd find the spot of earth that was partial to the man, that draws and holds him like a magnet."

Angus MacLeod was interrupted by one clear ring of the farm bell. The sound of the bell seemed to hang over the soft white fields, reluctant to roll away and away over the pitch of the mountain.

"We'll have to go," the man said to the boy. "Your grandmother hasn't had to call us to supper since harvest. She'll wonder what's become of us."

This too had been a harvest for the man, a gathering in of dreams and visions. From the white and frozen crust the warm dark earth had come to him. He had felt soft April rain drive him to shelter from making deep brown furrows. He had wiped the sweat from his brow in the long corn rows. He had stood in the golden grain field, whose waves rolled in the breeze, swinging to the rhythm of the eternal theme of nature's constancy.

Here in this spot the cold wind, the hidden frozen wagon ruts, the effortless low-slanted rays of the sun had lost their meaning, and winter's dark lifelessness had disappeared. In the heart of the man they had been replaced by the vast primeval hope of spring, rebirth, and resurrection. A sky as cold as steel had warmed. The honed edge of a steel-blue sky had filled with soft April clouds, sweeping the tops of the hills and brushing the earth with life.

"It's way past chore time," Una MacLeod said as the man and boy kicked the snow from their boots against the doorsill. "Where have you been?"

The boy and the man stood on the hearth with their backs to the fire, rubbing their hands behind them.

"Talking to the fields," the boy replied.

❧ Seven ❧

As the days passed, Tor grew more and more impatient. His grandfather's Black-faced Highlands already had so many lambs that he had to count the marks scratched on the shed wall to total up the number. Almost every day as the sheep wandered in at grain time, several ewes would be hanging back so that newborn lambs could keep up.

When Tor thought of keeping his four prize Cheviots in the shed, his grandpa had said, "It's better for the lambs if they're born in some sunny spot by a stone wall. And the ewe will find the warmest place. This time of year it's much warmer outside when the sun is high than in the shed. The sun's bringing out more new green every day, and there's nothing like new grass to get plenty of milk ready for when your lambs do come. They're finding more to nibble too. They're not even in any hurry to get to the grain trough."

"But these are my own first lambs," Tor would interrupt. "Why do all yours have to be born first?"

"Any day now," Angus MacLeod would answer, putting his hand on the boy's shoulder as they leaned against the shed gate, "you'll have four, maybe six. Sometimes Cheviots have twins their first lambing. Cheviots are born small, but they're active and tough. They're on their feet and getting milk in half the time it takes most breeds."

Finally a day came that set Tor's heartbeat racing. When the flock came in long after sundown, he counted only three of his ewes among his grandfather's many. He climbed the shed gate and counted again. When he was sure one was missing, he found Angus in the barn and said, "One's lambed. She didn't come in."

Halfway across the night pasture in search of the missing ewe Angus MacLeod was falling behind the boy and dog. Maybe Tor wanted to handle this alone.

"You don't have to come with me," the boy called without looking back. He had already repeated the same thing several times since they had left the barn.

The man now realized that he was out of place. The joy of finding his first lamb was something a boy would rather not share with anyone. Angus MacLeod understood. "Are you sure?" he called after the boy.

"I'm sure," the boy called without slackening his ever-quickening strides. The man watched until the boy had disappeared around the corner of the wall beyond the night pasture. He measured the amount of daylight left the boy, then made his way back past the barn to the kitchen.

"Should you have let him go alone?" Una MacLeod asked Angus when she had heard why Tor had not come in with him.

"He'll be all right," Angus replied. "I started with him, but by the time we were halfway across the night pasture he and Shep were fifty yards in front. He had said about a half dozen times, 'You don't have to go with me.' It finally dawned on me that this was no ordinary venture. He was going to find his very own first lamb. When he's telling the story on the school bus tomorrow, he won't have to say 'me and Grandpa.' He'll say 'I' like a real shepherd."

Una MacLeod glanced at the wall rack by the kitchen door. "He never remembers to change his good Mackinaw and school boots. I hope he doesn't come home carrying a wet lamb in his arms with that good jacket."

"He'll be careful. Besides, they can't be too far. The Indian mound pasture and the high meadow have been closed off since last fall. When I was a boy and Half-faced John's cabin hadn't fallen down, I used to have to find one up there occasionally. Pa said the sun was warmer there at the bottom of the cliffs than anywhere else on the mountain.

"I used to think I could still hear old John whistling 'Tenting Tonight on the Old Campground' the way Pa said he whistled it. He'd been dead for years. But the wind whistling in the crevices of the cliffs was old John, to me.

"But Pa used to send me up. He'd say, 'What man having a hundred sheep and having lost one did not leave the ninety and nine and go to find that which was lost?' "

Tor saw his grandfather disappear behind the kitchen door far below. He circled the fields with confidence. He searched along the walls. He startled a fox sparrow from its busy scratching in winter's dead grass and leaves. He put up a covey of bobwhites that had already gone to roost in their tight circle on the ground. They rose with a great flutter in all directions. He sent Shep to search the swales and the far side of knolls. Intermittently he called, "Rachel, Rachel." His grandfather had told him that this was the Old Testament name for little ewe.

Now the bobwhites Tor had scattered began to call each other from all directions to reassemble for the night. It was their covey call, rather plaintive, with a touch of mysterious lure.

At last he was approaching the entrance to the Indian mound pasture and the high meadow. The strip of orange-red above the Alleghenies was narrowing fast and fading into a dark magenta. Shep had returned from searching the last swales which were fast filling with purple. Tor was beginning to worry. He had kept a pace which had made Shep trot at intervals when he returned from his knoll and swale assignments and moved beside the boy.

But now Tor ceased his calling and stood listening. No hurry or worry was great enough to keep him from standing still to hear the winsome, bewitching "Bobwhite, bobwhite, is your wheat ripe?" that came to him. It seemed to soften the land and brighten the western sky's fading glow. Sometimes after it had been repeated three times the caller would add, "More wet, more wet." This in summer would bring his grandfather up short, and he would say, "He's calling for rain."

When there were only two or three stragglers

left answering each other with "Bobwhite, bob-white," Tor walked on, but at a less hurried step. By the time he reached the gate to the Indian mound pasture all was quiet. He knew the birds were back on the ground in their compact little circle, wing to wing, tails in and heads out, so each could take off "like shot out of a cannon," as Grandpa said. "It takes a smart fox to get one."

Years of sliding to and fro, or the rattling of the wooden bolt by summer's breeze and winter's wind, had worn the edges from the bolt slot so that the gate had been opened either by the wind or some thoughtless hunter.

Tor had gone with his grandfather to look for lost heifers often enough to have learned to look for tracks. In the gateway he found them—one set of sheep tracks going into the Indian mound pasture and the high meadow. These were two separate fields, but they served as a single summer pasture for sheep and young cattle. So Tor knew the barway between them was always open. They covered a great expanse of acreage, running north all the way to the base of the cliffs of the Hanging Gardens. His grandfather always used a horse when checking the stock here in summer.

Tor knew it was the nature of all animals to give birth to their young in as much privacy as they could find. "They'll go as far as they can," his grandpa always said. "They'll go to the highest spot so they can keep an eye out for the approach of an enemy. This is a carry-over from the days when they were wild."

Tor found himself repeating his grandfather's words aloud. Shep thought he was talking to him.

He wagged his tail and moved around to where he could look up into the boy's eyes as if to question, "What do you want me to do now?"

Tor looked back over the gentle slanted and rolling fields he had crossed. It had grown dark enough now so he could see the lighted windows of the kitchen far away. The evening star glimmered just above the mountains in the west.

He wished he had not come alone. If he had known the gate would be open, he would have ridden Little Sorrel, the horse his grandfather had named for Stonewall Jackson's famous war-horse. He tried to pick out the cliffs at the end of the upland. The distance and the dark cut them off; they were too far away.

He'd better go back and get his grandpa with a lantern, he thought. Maybe his ewe was still trying to have the lamb. She wouldn't be making a sound. He couldn't find her in the dark. The March wind was beginning to sweep the land. It was cold. Maybe the lamb would be chilled and die if he took time to go back for his grandfather. Sometimes ewes have trouble with their first lamb. Maybe his ewe was dead, and the lamb dead, still inside her.

If the lamb had been born and was all right, he could find them in the dark. The mother would bleat about every twenty minutes for the lamb to rise on its wobbly legs and get milk. He would listen in one spot and then move on to another and listen again.

If he went back, his grandmother would say, "You're chilled through and through, child. Eat your supper and do your schoolwork. Your grandfather will ride Little Sorrel up and look."

And worst of all, Grandpa might say, "You'll never find one ewe in that high meadow tonight. Sometimes it's hard enough to find a whole flock in the daytime. A lamb won't freeze outside tonight. What's happened has happened. We might as well wait 'til morning."

Tor rubbed his hand over the head of Shep for a long time. He patted him gently. Finally he spoke. "We'll go on, Shep." And boy and dog turned from looking back at the faraway glow of the kitchen window, a dim speck, the only light that showed on the whole horizon, and headed north into the backland.

He picked out the stars in the handle of the Big Dipper. The evening star had seemed near and flaming-warm. The stars in the handle of the Big Dipper now appeared far away and starkly cold.

The boy sent the dog in one direction and then another with the command, "Find the sheep, Shep."

As they approached the Indian mound, he kept the dog by his side. His grandfather had told him the mound was where the Monacan Indians had lived. They were a small branch of the Cherokee tribe, and this was the site of their "long house," where they held tribal council meetings. They had once lived farther south along Cedar Creek and the Lost River near Natural Bridge, which they called the Bridge of God. When they had been driven from the valley land, they had moved into the mountains. In time they had been driven westward across the mountains, finally ending up on far western desert land which no one else wanted. Tor wondered how many chiefs were buried in the mound. He stopped and listened to the distant "Who, whoo, who-oo cooks for you" of a great horned owl. It sounded like the signal whoop of an Indian. It was answered by the mournful whistle of a screech owl, rising to a tremulous cry, then falling to a low plaintive wail. Grandpa called it the shivers owl. Said it ran shivers up and down your spine. Shep's tail tapping the ground sounded like a muffled drumbeat. Tor ran his hand over Shep's head. This only made the drumbeat louder.

Past the Indian mound, Tor quickened his pace. The call of the bobwhite had said stay and listen; but there was something in the night cry of the owls which said hurry.

Shep covered the directions where the boy pointed. Tor listened for an excited bark which would tell him that his sheep was found. But each time Shep returned as quietly as he went. The light in the kitchen windows had fallen below Tor's view. He wished he would see a lantern crossing the fields below; that would help him keep his directions.

Back in the kitchen Una MacLeod was putting the boy's supper in the warming closet of the stove. Angus stood in the kitchen door listening.

"You must get the lantern and go and help him," Una MacLeod repeated with more determination than the time before. She had said it several times.

"I'll go," Angus replied. "But it's a great adventure for the boy. Pa used to send me out with a feed sack to carry the lambs home in. I forgot to tell Tor to take one. I'll give him a little more time. He knows sheep. If the lamb hadn't been born long, he'll wait to let it get first milk before he disturbs them. That's important. The moon'll be up soon and it's full, the planter's moon. Time to get the ground ready for planting as soon as it dries out."

Angus had lighted the fire in the fireplace to take the chill off. He closed the kitchen door and sat by the fire. Una noticed that he did not remove his boots. She was glad.

Tor missed the gap that led from the Indian mound pasture into the high meadow. He finally remembered that it was at the crown of a knoll, so he followed the stone wall uphill until he came to it. He had only missed it by a few yards. For an instant he was proud of himself. He would tell Grandpa that he was almost as good as him about finding his way over the land.

He stood at the gap and called, "Rachel, Rachel," in all directions. When he did it facing the Big Dipper, a faint echo came back to him. He knew that was the direction of the cliffs and the woodland. His voice had echoed off the cliffs. He repeated his grandpa's words to Shep, "They'll go as far as they can, hide in the brush or woods if they can."

The thought of going all the way to the cliffs and the woods sent more shivers up his spine than the screech owl had. He called Shep to his side. If he went to the cliffs, he would have to pass the spot where Half-faced John, the hermit, had lived and the tree where he had hanged himself; and no one had found him until the buzzards had picked his bones clean.

Grandpa had told him the story, and he had told it in history class at school. But the teacher had made him stop when he came to the part about how Grandpa MacLeod's father had found the skeleton hanging with the legs pulled off by varmints or something.

Half-faced John had been a soldier in the Northern Army during the Civil War. His real name was John Payne, and Grandpa said he was the brother of one of the men who had conspired to shoot Abraham Lincoln. At the Battle of Slaughter Mountain, over near Gordonsville, he had the whole side of his face burned and one eye put out, by gunpowder, trying to blow up the Orange-Culpeper railroad.

When he saw what an awful sight he was, with one side of his face all swiveled and red and his sightless eye solid white, he left the camp hospital and wandered into the mountains to hide and die. Grandpa's father had found him living up under the cliffs like a wild man. He let him build a cabin on the land, and paid him for cutting wood and brush. Sometimes he used to come to the barn; but he'd never go to the house. Never wanted any children or womenfolk to see him. But Grandpa had hid in the barn as a boy and seen him lots of times.

They said he used to go off the mountain at night and knock on the storekeeper's door to get provisions. He used to go away for months at a time. Grandpa said he went by the mountains back to where he'd come from. Said he'd watch in the woods around where he'd lived to see his loved ones, but never went out to let them see him.

Then one time when he hadn't been seen for a while, Grandpa's father found his skeleton hanging from a tree near the cabin, with his clothes still on him, hanging in tatters, and his leg bones pulled off. Grandpa said his pa wouldn't let him go with him when he went and buried him near his cabin, so he didn't know where the grave was.

Tor had seen the tree. He hoped he wouldn't have to go that far. He searched the horizon for a moving lantern, but there was none.

While he had been shivering at the thoughts of Half-faced John, a small arc of gold had appeared above the far mountains. In no time at all it was a half circle. Then it was a great bright disk, clearing the mountain, climbing up the sky. By its light Tor could see the stone walls that ran down the ridge. Far in the distance he could see the outline of the cliffs against the sky.

From somewhere on the mountain, a fox barked at the moon. Tor remembered that his grandpa said they'd never bark when they were hungry. But when they'd feasted on a rabbit or something, they'd sit on their haunches and bay at the moon just like a dog.

Tor suddenly realized that Shep had disappeared on his own. Was it the fox or had he scented the ewe? Tor wondered if the fox might not have feasted on his lamb. No, the mother would butt the daylights out of the fox. Tor whistled for his dog. A faint echo came back from the faraway cliffs. The echo sounded like somebody had whistled a soft tune. It was a tune he had never heard before. Half-faced John had always whistled "Tenting Tonight on the Old Campground." Tor wondered what that tune sounded like. "An echo runs things together," he said aloud. "No use to be afraid of anything about the dead."

Shep came bounding back from the direction of the woodland. With the moon up, Tor felt much braver. "There's no such thing as a ghost of Half-faced John or Indians either," he said aloud to Shep. "It's living varmints that we have to worry about," he added, as he heard the bark of the fox again, much closer. Shep stopped and pricked up his ears. "No, Shep," the boy said. Shep dropped back to walk with him.

Tor found himself veering toward the corner of the high meadow which would keep him from passing the site of Half-faced John's cabin and the hanging tree. He pointed for Shep to search in that direction. He would go to the top of the last rise and wait for Shep. The stone wall that bordered the high meadow ran just inside the woods. He would stay out in the moonlight and let Shep go into the dark under the hemlocks.

Once long ago, when he was only five or six, his grandpa had shown him one of the trees with great strips of its bark torn off. "A killer bear testing his strength," his grandfather had said. He had probably gotten a whiff of the sheep or cattle, his grandfather had explained, and that had whetted his appetite for the kill. So he tested his claws on the tree. But a bear could never catch sheep in the open. Only if he got the sheep in a corner and they were scared stiff with fright. Then he would maul them to death. Grandpa had found three of his

Black-faced Highlands mangled and one half-eaten in the hemlock corner. "But that was before you were born," his grandfather had said.

Shep returned from searching and gave the boy the same disappointed look. Tor felt a little relief that he hadn't barked and wagged his tail and set off in the direction from which he had come. That would mean he had found the sheep somewhere near the hanging tree. Relieved, Tor now pointed in the direction of the hemlock corner, wondering if he'd feel any better about going in if Shep found her there.

There were still bears in the mountain, even if they hadn't killed any sheep for years. Tor had read in the paper about hunters shooting them, but not so much on his mountains as across the valley in the Alleghenies.

Shep had scarcely started toward the dark woods when Tor heard a sharp clipped bark. The dog was back in an instant, wagging his tail and barking. Tor quieted the dog and moved very cautiously in the direction Shep led. Misgivings replaced the instant excitement he had enjoyed at hearing Shep's bark. They were still in the open. She wouldn't have had her lamb here. Shep moved ahead quietly as Tor had ordered. Tor peered through the moonlight, pausing with every step to listen.

After not more than a dozen steps it came to him—the rapid thump, thump, thump of a sheep stomping her foot. Tor picked up Shep's dark form in the moonlight. And there right in front of him was the ewe. Tor moved closer and saw a white ball directly under her. She stomped her foot at the dog and boy, but moved to one side, then turned and put her nose against the white ball and bleated. The white ball divided in half; each half bounced in a different direction.

Tor could scarcely believe his eyes or the action which followed. His ewe had twins. He had thought only in terms of one tiny new lamb, still wobbly on its rubbery legs.

In the barn lot his ewes were so tame he could rub his hand over the soft wool, scratch their heads, and they would follow him, asking for more. Now the ewe was wild, moving in a circle, trying to keep her lambs together and away from boy and dog. The lambs were several hours old and, as was characteristic of Cheviots, quite capable of trying to keep out of reach of the stranger who had just appeared. Shep moved in a wide arc outside the circle of ewe, lambs, and boy.

Tor tried to turn the ewe in the direction of home, but she would not lose sight of her lambs. She walked backward or circled or went from side to side. When the boy realized that they were getting nowhere, he caught the lambs and held them in his arms. Now the mother moved back and forth in front of him, never letting the lambs out of her sight. The lambs squirmed in his arms. When the ewe had run under his feet and he had tripped and nearly fallen on the lambs several times, he decided there had to be a better way.

He had seen his grandfather walking calmly, a grain sack over his shoulder with two woolly heads sticking out of slits he had made in the sack, and the ewe walking behind, bleating as she followed. "Why didn't we remember to bring a grain sack?" Tor spoke aloud to Shep, who was still staying well out of the way.

One lamb squirmed free and bounced off its mother's back to the ground as she darted in front of Tor. He was afraid to squeeze the other tight enough to hold it. So he put it gently on the ground.

He began to unbutton his Mackinaw. He would tie it into a bag and carry them that way. He felt in his pockets for string. He always had several pieces. But tonight, when he needed it for something far more important than tying rubber bands on a pronged stick to make a gravel shooter, he had none.

For the first time during the whole night he began to sniffle. He blew his nose, and an idea was born. Better than tying his Mackinaw into a bag, he would cut his handkerchief in half, tie the end of each sleeve, put a lamb in each, with its head sticking out, and carry them on his back. "The way Indians would carry papooses," he said to Shep. He cut the hem of the handkerchief with his knife and ripped it the rest of the way. He was already cold without his jacket, but that didn't matter.

It worked. With boy and lambs and jacket on the ground in a heap, the frantic mother dancing wildly, Tor stuffed one lamb in tailfirst, held his knee on it while he got the other in, hung them low over his back so the mother could see them, and started for home. The ewe followed on his heels, bleating with each step. Shep dropped behind to drive but found that unnecessary. His only problem was keeping up.

Halfway across the Indian mound pasture Tor saw the moving light of a lantern far below on the horizon. He was no longer cold. He heard no drumbeats as he passed the Indian mound. The moonlight on the fields and the bleating of his ewe brought the world alive and made it beautiful.

When man and boy came together, the man held the lantern high and studied the boy's precious burden. "How'd you ever think of that," he asked, "and how'd she ever get into the upper land?"

"The gate was open," the boy replied. And after a long pause he added, "On the way up I was thinking of Indians, so I thought of this."

"Want me to carry them the rest of the way?"

"No, they aren't a bit heavy."

The man thought of taking his jacket off to put around the boy. But then he thought better and didn't. Instead he blew out the lantern.

Over the fields drenched in moonlight, a man and a boy walked in silence. The thoughts of each too meaningful for words, one too wise, the other too happy.

At the barn Angus MacLeod lit the lantern and hung it on a peg. He spread new bedding in one of the lambing pens. Tor unloaded his lambs and exclaimed with great pleasure, "They're both ewes. I can keep them to increase my flock."

He brushed his jacket carefully, smelling each sleeve before he put it on and buttoned it. Grandmother would never know he had used it for a lamb cradle.

In the kitchen Tor ate his supper for the first

time in his life at ten o'clock in the night. He thought his grandmother would say something about schoolwork, but she didn't. But while he was eating, she had repeated three times, "We were worried sick. I told your grandfather he should go find you."

The first two times she said it, Angus MacLeod just poked at the log on the fire and said nothing. When she said it the third time, Angus stood up and leaned against the stone mantelpiece. "I wasn't worried at all," he said. Tor noticed tears in his grandmother's eyes. But Grandpa was smiling.

Tor wondered if this would be a good time to start some more talk about getting a big red tractor, except it was too late. He would save it for tomorrow or the next day. Grandpa would still remember that he wasn't such a kid anymore. So he gave Shep the four meatless spareribs from his plate, said good night, and went to bed. The toe of each boot scraped on the edge of each stairstep as he went. His boots had got very heavy.

By the time he got home from school the next day his boots had got light again. So he jumped off the bus with his usual wide stride, barely touching the bus step.

He had looked for someone at school to tell about his hunt for his lost sheep and his new lambs. He thought that he might tell Martha Hillyer, but then he remembered that she had Southdown sheep and was always saying how much better Southdowns were than Cheviots. So nobody seemed just right to hear it, not even his teacher.

Besides, Tor was inclined to agree with his grandpa, who said, "Some stories are too good to be told."

Shep was at the mailbox. Tor greeted him with a question: "Find any new lambs today, Shep?" Other than Grandpa and Grandmother, Tor would rather talk to Shep than almost anybody else he knew. Shep always seemed to understand.

"I rode up and fixed the Indian mound pasture gate latch before I turned the sheep out," Angus MacLeod began as Tor took his place at the table in front of a brimming bowl of soup, with three biscuits by its side. His grandmother had it ready by the time he got his jacket off. "I rode on up to the high meadow and Shep smelled out the place where your lambs had been born. Right in the darkest corner of the hemlock grove on a nice soft bed of hemlock needles. But the rise where you found your ewe is higher ground than where they were born. So she brought them out there for the night. From there she could see any enemy approaching from all sides. Instinct from ages ago when they were wild and didn't have good shepherds like you to look after them."

"Any more lambs today, are mine all right?" Tor asked with a single breath.

"Yours are as spry as crickets. Three Black-faced Highlands looked droopy, so I kept them in. They each had a single. I guess you took all my luck for twins."

"Do you think I might get more twins?"

"Could," his grandfather replied and added, "Once they start, they drop by the dozen. There might have been more in the fields today."

"Then be sure not to wait until dark to start looking," Una MacLeod ordered.

"And we'll have to look every day now," Angus said, "because I can't count two hundred Black-faced Highlands coming through the gate."

Long before sunset the man, boy, and dog were following the sheep across the fields toward the barn. Five ewes, with lambs trailing, came behind the main flock. All were Black-faced Highlands. When the ewes and new lambs had been bedded down for the night, the man and boy sat on the railing of the lambing pen and watched long enough to be sure all the lambs were getting milk. There were two sets of twins and three singles. Tor could see that Grandpa had had a good day.

"It's about time for the Farm Bureau salesman to come around," Tor ventured.

"Yes, I've got seed corn ordered. That's all I need, but he'll be peddling all kinds of gadgets."

"Do you think you might buy a tractor this year, Grandpa?" Tor came right to the point. "It would save a lot of work and time. Everybody has one."

"You'd make a good salesman, Tor. That's exactly what they say, 'It would save work and time.' But not everybody has one. Those Mennonite farmers down in the valley, with the best crops, the smoothest fields and cleanest fence rows in the county, don't have tractors. And some of them even have big crop farms. It's different with us. We have a grazing farm. We only plant what we need to feed ourselves and our stock."

Angus MacLeod liked to see the land left green and the earth held firm with heavy sod if it wasn't really needed for sown crops. He thought men went crazy when they got hold of big machinery, planting more than they could use or sell, ruining the country for the farmer, having the government pay them for plowing and not planting. Then letting the soil lie brown and sterile or dry out and blow away as dust.

"When the tractor salesman talks about saving work and time," the man continued quietly, "I say I don't want to be saved from work I enjoy. You'll learn what I mean when you're a little bigger and can walk behind a plow in a deep furrow or follow a cultivator through rows of corn whose blades keep the horseflies and gnats brushed away as you go."

To Angus MacLeod it would have seemed almost sinful to plow without feeling the soft earth under his feet. There was something he couldn't describe to the boy about a team of plow horses; two if the sod was light or fallow cornland to go back to grass, three if the sod was heavy, walking together, leaning gently against traces and single-tree. Only a man following could know how carefully they seemed to part the earth and fold it gently over, never tearing it the way a tractor did. Then, too, tractors left scars everywhere—ruts in lanes and barn lots. The wheels ribbed and pocked the sod of whatever field they crossed.

Angus MacLeod was looking through the open door of the shed, past the edge of his land and the rim of the mountain. He seemed lost in thought. Tor couldn't really think of anything to say to fill up the long pauses. He liked to listen to his grandfather. Now he didn't know whether he was glad or sorry he had brought up the tractor subject. And the man, too, was trying to think of words to speak his feeling.

"All this talk about saving time that they bring up," Angus continued. "I ask them, 'Time for what?' Time to go to the bank once a month to make the payment on the tractor. Time to run to town for new parts because something is always breaking. Time to tinker with whatever always needs adjusting or replacing. Time to go to auctions and buy what you don't need, or go to town and sit on the courthouse square and talk about the weather and politics, being able to do nothing about either. That shuts them up."

Deep in his heart Angus MacLeod knew the Almighty who gave him the land provided "A time to plant and a time to gather in what is planted." And no man could hurry either. A man following a team the length of a long upland meadow to the quiet music of one firmly planted hoof after another learned that time could not be saved—that time was running a fast race even at the snail's pace of a man trailing behind a plow.

Besides, tractors would bring the smell of gasoline and exhaust fumes, and they would destroy the smells of a field in spring. Angus MacLeod liked the whiff of horse dandruff from a mane tossed by the wind. The smell of wet leather from a collar hugging a foamy neck. The reassuring smell of strength from sweaty flanks rubbed by tight traces and loose guiding lines. The scent of organic earth and wild garlic turned up to the sun.

And smells that teach a lesson—the smell of stagnation and decay in a field mouse's nest with four tiny skeletons uncovered—the lesson of nature's great mysteries in her smallest creatures.

Tractors would drown out the sounds a man likes to hear in the fields. The rattle of the stubble and dead stalks as a plow buries them. The sound of dark earth slipping over the moldboard. The sound of the plow point exploring the size of a stone or the dimension of a root. The sound of a turned furrow pillowing against one already plowed. The noisy chirp of an excited robin refusing to share a worm. The creak of the depth wheel and the sharp cut of the coulter. The whine of the hitch—beam to singletree, singletree to trace. The flick of a line against a lagging flank and the clank of a bit in a restless mouth. The cadenced rhythm of one hoof set after another. The deep exhaling from dilated nostrils at the end of the furrow, and the soft voice of the plowman ordering the turn or the "Whoa" for rest.

Riding a tractor, a man would never catch the faraway "honk, honk," of wild geese moving north or learn the wisdom of their certain flight. He would miss the first notes of the song sparrow, claiming a spot in some distant fence row for his own. Why, he would even miss the bell that calls him home.

Angus MacLeod knew that a man needs to smell and hear to keep him remembering that he belongs to the earth as much as the earth belongs to him. When he can walk close to it, the soil prepares him as he prepares the soil. As the last coolness of winter is turned up to the sun to be warmed out, so the last of winter's chill leaves the man—he gets it out of his bones. He plows part of the soil, its warmth, its hope, its life, into his own soul. But how could he tell all this to the boy?

The sun was gone now. Una MacLeod had grown impatient. The farm bell signaled suppertime. Angus MacLeod studied the boy as he stood aside and let his dog and grandfather go through the shed door, then pulled the wide door tight and latched it.

"Maybe we could buy a little cub tractor that you could use to mow the grass around the house and in the orchard," Angus said as he walked. "But I'd miss the sheep grazing and the tinkle of their bells to put me to sleep at night."

While his grandfather scraped his boots at the doorstep, Tor was taking one last look at a gold-edged cloud above the mountain, all that was left of a day. "I guess we don't need a cub tractor, Grandpa. I'd rather hear the bells, too."

⚸ Eight ⚸

At the supper table, where they arrived late because of Angus' refusal to let time and tractors hurry him, Tor MacLeod asked, "Grandpa, how come you got a truck and a car since you hate machinery so much?"

"I really don't know," his grandfather answered after a long pause. "I guess it was because with more and more cars on the road to endanger horses, I did it for their sake. But I always wish I hadn't when I see my Mennonite friends driving to the Farm Bureau picnic in their buggies and surreys."

"Now tell the truth, Angus," Una MacLeod interrupted. "You know it was the boys, Torm and Logan. They hounded and pestered from the time they were Tor's age. And now I'm so thankful you—" Tor's grandmother left the sentence unfinished and got up to look after something on the stove. Tor noticed that she raised her apron and wiped her eyes.

"Well, a truck was right useful, and the car is nice for church. The boys always used the car a lot. Then when your pa was married, he had one of his own." Angus noticed Una, too, and said no more.

"You won't ever have a telephone, will you, Grandpa?"

"Never! Does a man more injury than a tractor. Makes him a slave. I've been at the bank or people's houses, and if it rings, they'll stop right in the middle of a sentence, or drop whatever they're doing, to answer it. Why, I've been sitting on Hillyer's veranda with him and Mrs. Hillyer, and when that thing would ring, she'd be out of her rocker like somebody had yelled 'Fire,' slamming the screen door behind her, to get to that thing. And when she'd come back and Hillyer would ask her what it was, she'd say Mrs. Dudley just called to say that one of the Smith children punched Dudley's dog in the eye, and the dog bit it. That they'd have to have the dog tested to see if it had rabies. Not a word though about having the child tested for savagery. Or some other rigmarole like whose baby was born and what it was named. Or who had been elected president of the Altar Guild in the church but wasn't a fit person to serve. Half the time a telephone rings, it's somebody begging for some cause or some salesman, too lazy to move from a swivel chair, trying to sell something."

"But sometimes it might be important," Tor insisted.

"Then whatever the message is, it gets to you soon enough. If it's bad news, it travels too fast, and if it's good news, it's worth waiting for the mailman to bring."

Tor made no further attempts to modernize his grandfather. But he watched closely to see if time would not outrun him.

Before March was over, the ground had dried

out. Grandpa was no longer in the kitchen or tinkering at the woodshed or barn when Tor came from school. He was in the fields. Now Tor did almost all the chores before his grandfather came in at sundown.

By the time the dogwoods and redbud bloomed along the fence rows and at the edge of the woods, Tor's Cheviots had given him another set of twins and two singles.

"Beginner's luck," Grandpa said. But Grandpa's Black-faced Highlands had more lambs than Tor could count. "Almost three hundred," Angus said.

The grass was green enough and the nights warm, too, so the sheep no longer had to be penned at night. Tor asked his grandfather if he could graze his Cheviots in the graveyard, and Angus said, "Yes. So you can count them every day."

When Angus stretched himself and yawned after supper, Una would say, "Spring is the busiest time of the year."

And Angus would come right back with, "The best time of the year."

One night Angus announced, "The oats are all planted, and just at the right time—when the pink begins to show in the apple buds. The corn land is plowed, but I can't plant it yet. Have to wait 'til the oak leaves are as big as a squirrel's ear."

Tor didn't say anything, but he understood. Time and his grandfather were moving through the fields together, with Grandpa still just a few steps ahead.

Tor's mother wanted him to come to the city for Easter. But Tor wrote that there was too much spring work. So his mother and stepfather came to the mountain. They brought eight Swiss sheep bells, which Tor liked; now he had bells for all his sheep. They brought him a new suit, which he didn't like but didn't say anything. He was used to his old suit. His grandmother had to lengthen the pants of his new suit by making French cuffs. He had grown more than his mother had estimated.

Tor wished school ended in April. He needed more time to get things done. He couldn't understand it. He still had the same chores, and the days were longer, but he needed more time. He didn't realize that in April and May a boy needs more time to turn over rocks along a brook and discover things or just stand in the sun and listen.

The meadowlarks had gone from the barn lot to the fields, and more had come from the south. They flew low over the ground, their golden V-shaped wings alternating between frolicsome flutter and motionless sailing. Their white outer tail feathers opened and closed with a nervous flick as they flew. And always singing. Whether in flight or perched atop a stone wall, their high-pitched whistled "To-see-you, to-see-you, to-see-her, to-see-her-her-her" competed with the bobwhites and bobolinks.

Tor had learned from watching his grandfather that to hear is one thing, and one can hear and keep walking; but to listen is something else. "A man has to stop to listen," his grandpa always said, "to let the feeling catch up and soak in." So this was the time of year when Tor had to spend a lot of time listening.

The meadowlarks, the bobwhites, and the bobolinks were the birds of the fields. From rail and post the bobwhite increased in both volume and number his "Bobwhite, bobwhite, bobwhite, is your wheat ripe? Is your wheat ripe? Is your wheat ripe? More wet, more-wet, more-wet." But however much he tried, he could not outdo the bobolink's bubbling notes, tumbling over each other: "Bobolink, bobolink, spink, spank, spink, old geezer, old geezer, old geezer," like a music box with its mainspring run wild, about to explode. Only the scream of a chicken hawk, made bold by hunger, moved down from riding April clouds to circle the fields, stopped all song and helped a boy remember that he must bring home the cows.

Almost too fast for a boy to keep up, spring raced, panting her perfumed breath of apple blossoms and alfalfa clover over the green carpet of April and May, into summer. An artist from the town came and asked permission to paint the mountain scene. Angus, who had lived with the land and the sky so long that the picture was a part of him, said, "Go ahead. But I doubt if it's much that anybody would like to look at."

Tor checked on the progress of the picture each day when he came from school. When it was finished, he told his grandfather the artist, Mr. Benson, would sell it for a hundred and fifty dollars if he could reserve the right to borrow it for art shows.

"For a hundred and fifty dollars I can buy a good breed cow," was Angus' reply. "Besides, I know what the old place looks like."

"But if we hung it over the mantel, we could

look at the apple blossoms and green fields when the wind howls in winter," Tor argued.

Una MacLeod also thought it would be nice to have. "It would take all my egg money for a whole year. He'll still have it. Maybe you'll want to buy it sometime, when you'll be selling surplus lambs," she said to Tor.

School was finally over, and Tor was free to follow his grandfather through the long summer days. He was also free from worry about having to go back to the city. His mother was at last convinced that his happiness was here, with his grandfather, on the MacLeod place. She brought a new bicycle early in the summer.

He learned to handle a quiet team of workhorses alongside his grandfather in the fields. He often rode his bike to David Hillyer's swimming hole. Not that David's was any better than his own; but a lot of the time he didn't swim at all. Instead he drove one of the tractors in the fields with David and his father. He even learned to drive the big flatbed truck to gather the baled hay. When they did go to the swimming hole, David Hillyer threw rocks at Martha if she tried to follow.

The days ran into seasons, the seasons into years. Tor found himself impatient with time's erratic movement. It either moved too fast or too slow. Except for chore time, winter and school moved at a snail's pace. But summer raced from May to September faster than a scared rabbit or water over a slick rock. If Tor was waiting for lambs to be born, time was too slow; if he was showing them at the county fair and sleeping on a bale of hay in the exhibit pen, the time raced by before he had seen half the things he wanted to see at the fair. The time needed for a sapling to grow into a tree and bear fruit, for seeds to grow into a harvest, was too great for him to measure and made him impatient. But not his grandfather. The boy wondered how the man, never hurrying, was always ready for a new season and a new year.

It was about the middle of Tor's fourth summer that a passing remark of the manager of the Farm Bureau, as he lifted a bag of cattle salt into the back of Angus' truck, crashed like "a thunderclap with the sun shining" upon the ears of Angus Mac-Leod.

"After all these years of rumor and delay since the war, I hear it's final that the government is starting to move ahead again on the Skyland Parkway. Going to extend it all the way to Eagle's Aerie. I wish I had some of that mountain land to sell them. You people up there will get a good price."

"That rumor has gone around off and on ever since the end of the war," said Angus McLeod. "What would be the sense of building a road along the top of the mountain paralleling the acres of cement they've smothered and ruined the best land of the valley with? Acres and acres left useless between lanes and encircled by exits and entrances. Farms split in half so that a man might have to travel five miles to get to a field in sight of his house. How'd the rumor get started this time?"

Tor noticed that his grandfather's voice had risen to the point of aggravation.

"Somebody, and I've forgotten who it was, said Ernest Adair had a government bulletin on national forests and their accessibility by interstate and defense highways, and that it showed the whole mountaintop from Thornton's Gap to Eagle's Aerie as national forest with a highway along the top of the mountain. The whole section was marked 'Engineering and land acquisition in progress.' "

"That doesn't mean anything," Angus called back as he climbed into the truck and began to move it to let another customer back up to the loading platform. "Don't you know the government keeps hundreds of people busy making plans that change with each administration? They've ruined the valley. They can't destroy the mountain."

"What good's the highway from Bent Mountain to Thornton's Gap?" Tor asked when they were out of the street noise.

"No good. Except for sightseers. It doesn't go anywhere. It started out to be nothing but an access road to forestlands the government acquired during the big Depression of the nineteen thirties to make jobs for the Civilian Conservation Corps. But some scheming politician, wanting money spent in his district, promoted a scenic highway."

"You should have stopped at the bank and asked Mr. Adair. He's the president of the bank."

"Yes. I guess," Angus replied. "He lives on the mountain and has brought three mountain farms during the last four years. Maybe he *does* know something. But he's the kind of man I don't enjoy talking to. I always get the feeling that he's saying one thing but thinking another. Besides, he weighs two hundred and fifty pounds. His jowls hang over his shirt collar, and his paunch rolls over his belt halfway down to his knees. I think a man is a glutton when he lets himself get that way."

Tor offered no other suggestion. His grandfather repeated several times as though he hadn't heard himself, "From Thornton's Gap to Belvidere, and on to Montevideo. All the way to Eagle's Aerie."

The rest of the way home Angus was deep in thought. "If it does come," he said as they came in sight of his sky meadows, "it'll go to the west from Humpstack Gap to Fisher's Rock. That'll make a better grade, and it'll be a mile below our land. It wouldn't be sensible for them to pull it all the way up over our plateau. Besides, I'd never give them rights. From Bent Mountain to Thornton's Gap it went through worthless mountain land most of which the government had bought for five dollars an acre for a national forest. But the hundred and twenty miles from Thornton's Gap to Eagle's Aerie has at least thirty farms astride the ridge. I doubt if half a dozen of the owners would agree to sell. So they'll have to go around them.

"Those fellows who went through here last summer and several summers ago with their surveying equipment, sticking pegs all over the place, said they were getting elevations for a geodetic map. I doubted them then. Chances are they were lying. The government has a way of slipping in the back door; and they've got what they want before anybody realizes what's going on. I'll write my county assemblyman and congressman right away. I'll find out what's going on."

Tor listened in silence. His grandfather looked grim and worried. When he got out of the truck, he pulled himself up to the full height of a mountain man. He crossed the yard with the wide strides of a man harassed and angry. Tor almost had to run to keep up.

During the days that Angus waited for letters to come from the state capital and Washington, he talked a lot to Una at mealtime and on the porch, but in the fields he talked little. Tor found it hard to find something to talk about. His grandfather seemed to be thinking all the time. Often he would stand looking far away. Tor wished he would tell again, as he had so often when they worked together, how the fields came into being. So Tor was relieved one afternoon when five clear, measured tolls of the farm bell announced a visitor. But on the way from the fields he wondered if it would be someone with more bad news about the road.

His fears proved groundless. Rocking on the porch with his grandmother was Mr. Walter Johnston. "A remarkable man!" Angus called him. Tor liked him because he was always full of exciting stories.

"He's writing a story of the boys from this state who died in World War Two," Angus said as he waved from the far corner of the orchard.

"Why does he walk everywhere?" Tor asked.

"It's just his way. He showed up here years ago

when he was writing a story about Southerners who refused to fight in the Civil War. We hit it off, even though he's a relative of General Joseph E. Johnston, who didn't surrender until two weeks after Appomattox. Neither of us thinks war ever makes much sense. His older sister, Mary Johnston, was a writer too. She used some MacLeod history in her book called *To Have and to Hold*.

"He lives over at Warm Springs, but thinks nothing of walking sixty-five miles to use the university library. Once a year he goes to the state capital, walking the hundred and twenty miles both ways. He's walked all over the state to gather information for his story about the boys who died in the war. Tries to talk to people who were in the same battles with the ones who died. The Twenty-ninth Division took the first brunt of the battle at Omaha beachhead in the invasion. Five boys from the little town of Bedford alone died there.

"This is out of his way to the capital, but he always lays over a night going and coming. He is indeed a remarkable man!"

"I told Mrs. MacLeod not to call you from work," the sun-browned little man, whose gray hair stood in bold contrast to his weathered color, said as he moved toward Angus and Tor, taking a hand of each in his own. "Since I'm spending the night, and maybe the rest of the summer, there was no hurry."

"Welcome, welcome, welcome! Tor and I are always glad to be called from the fields. Tor'll bring some cool grape juice and we won't move from our rockers 'til milking time."

"I paced myself to get here after milking time,

but I must confess I weakened and accepted a ride. Clipped off quite a few of the valley pike miles in a buggy with one of your Mennonite farmer friends from Weyers Cave, a man named Menno Yoder. He says he knows you from the Farm Bureau picnic and seeing your livestock at the fair."

"I don't recall the name. I probably would if I saw him."

"He'd been down at Stuart's Draft for a few days helping out one of his friends who hurt his back. Seems a paper box flew out of a truck, caused his horse to shy, and his buggy turned over."

"They are great for neighborliness. And the best farmers anywhere, as I've often told Tor."

Tor and his grandmother went for grape juice and ginger cakes. By the time they returned, Angus had finished the small talk of weather and crops and was saying, "I've heard the rumble of distant thunder that'll bring a dark cloud to our mountain. There's talk that the government wants to extend the Skyland Parkway all the way from Thornton's Gap to Eagle's Aerie. I'm waiting for mail now from my assemblyman and congressman."

"I doubt if you have to worry," Walter Johnston mused after a long pause. "It'll be down to the west if it comes. They wouldn't climb up here."

"There were people surveying through here four or five summers ago, then again last summer. Drove stakes right up to the dooryard, which I pulled up as soon as they left. Said they were making a map. This is quite different from the Bent

Mountain-Thornton's Gap section. There were no mountain farms there. From here to Eagle's Aerie and back to Thornton's Gap there are at least thirty farms that would be broken up. The people won't stand for it."

"Your mountain road is one of the few pleasant ones left," said Walter Johnston. "It's not a joy to walk many places anymore. They are spreading concrete and asphalt over the whole country, it seems. They tear through the mountains and leave torn cuts and fills that'll never heal. They fill whole valleys with sprawling concrete pretzels so drivers can enter and exit at breakneck speed.

"Drivers screech to a stop and offer me rides when I'm walking in the open country and through the mountain. When I wave them on, they shake their heads. They think I'm crazy.

"I've taken rides with a truck driver now and again, thinking I might write a story about them sometime. They are very nice men. They are keenly aware of the lethal machines they have in their hands. They comment on the crazy drivers who risk their lives to get past them on the road. They talk of their families and tell you exactly when they'll get back home from their run. They point out some quiet little farm far to the side of the concrete desert and say that's what they want someday. They find friends wherever they stop, and they always want to buy you food and drink.

"They're generous dreamers who are slaves to the net of concrete that's spread over the land. They're aware of what's happening. Know all about the freight lobbyists in Washington who fight for the two percent grades responsible for all the scars left on the countryside by cuts and fills. Someday I'll get around to writing my story about *them*. Perhaps I should write about what the country will look like when a quarter of it is spread with concrete."

"That should be written," Angus replied, "and be sure to include how many people are harmed in the doing. Besides, there is the waste of good land about which nobody in authority seems to care. That's the one to write. By the way, how's your book on the war coming along?"

"I've gathered all the information, but as I try to write, I find myself asking the depressing questions that so many who fought asked me as I talked to them. 'What did we fight for? Where is peace if the most important thing in the world seems to be more machinery to destroy more of mankind?' I've come to agree with the great Greek writer Thucydides whose description of war still holds today. He said that while greed in the hearts of a few or a triviality may start a war, even the utter defeat of one side cannot really stop it. He said that the only peace that war and victory can bring is the peace of death, desolation, and a desert—social demoralization, intellectual confusion, political corruption, and economic ruin. He said he meant his story to be a lesson for men for all time."

"Men won't ever learn that lesson," Angus volunteered.

"The truth of his writing was too much even for his own people," said Walter Johnston. "He disappeared before he had a chance to finish his history. It is thought that political leaders of his day had him done away with. A few hundred years later a Roman named Tacitus put the same truth in a single sentence about his nation. He said, speaking of the Romans, 'They created a desert and called it peace.' Now I'm through preaching."

"And it's milking time," said Angus. "Come along to the barn with us."

"And I'll stir up something for supper while you're gone," Una MacLeod said, as the two men and Tor started for the barn.

Walter Johnston changed the subject to crops and land and weather. He hoped he could keep Angus off the subject of war for the rest of his stay. For of all the tragedies that come with war, he had found none more tragic than the one visited upon the MacLeods.

Walter Johnston had written the story of the MacLeods who would not fight to keep men enslaved in their southland during the War Between the States. He had compiled a paragraph or two which made Ross MacLeod, Angus' brother, one of a list, a statistic, of those who went far across the sea from their valley towns and their mountain farms to make the world safe for democracy in World War I.

He followed the man and his grandson about their evening chores. He had gathered the details of how the man's sons, Torm and Logan, had died to stop the march of a ravaging madman across the world. As he followed the man and boy, he wondered if he should write the story. Angus Mac-Leod had provided the details for Ross' story. The boy had read it, turned white, and sat statuelike for a long time. Half the story of Torm and Logan

MacLeod had come from a young man near Luray who had been in Captain Torm MacLeod's company. The other half had come from a lad who worked the gas pump at his service station in Five Forks, Virginia, with iron hooks for hands. He had flown with Logan MacLeod.

Thoughts of the stories he had gathered tormented him. He left the man and boy inside the barn for the longest chore of milking. He sat on the edge of the ancient stone watering trough. "If the boy," he said half aloud to himself, and continued in a whisper, "blanched and froze at the story of a great uncle he had never known, it would be cruel to write of how his father died. Better to leave the story official and stark in its brief form: Killed in action." If the story were written longer, the boy would close his door, shut out the world, read it, and, having finished, never be the same again.

Walter Johnston ran his index finger through the surface of the clear mountain water. Ripples formed. Then shapes and pictures made themselves from ripples.

❧ Nine ❧

As Angus MacLeod and his friend rocked and talked away the evening, Angus returned again and again to the threatened mutilation that would destroy his sky land if the rumors he had heard proved to be correct. Walter Johnston listened and studied his friend.

He hoped this man might not be harried out of the world he and his forebears had created.

Una MacLeod listened as the men talked. Several times she quietly reminded Angus that there was nothing certain about the road and that the rumor had cropped up off and on ever since the highway had been finished to Thornton's Gap.

Once when Angus said it would be the ruin of him, she interrupted, "In this life we learn to adjust, and it always seems too much for a human being to bear. But it almost never is."

Tor understood his grandfather's feelings, but he wished they would stop talking about the threat of the highway so Mr. Johnston would tell some of his stories.

His grandmother continued after a brief silence during which no one agreed that human nature was as flexible as she had made it out to be.

"I once watched a blind hen among my laying

chickens make a miraculous adjustment to her dark world and save herself. One season after molting a few new feathers on her neck came in red, bright and beautiful. Somewhere back in the breeding there had been some Rhode Island Red mixed with Plymouth Rock blood, I suppose. The gray Plymouth Rock hens began to peck at the red feathers. Chickens are vicious when they get started on a weak one or one that attracts them as being different.

"So before I realized it, they had blinded her. Then I noticed that the blind hen sat on the roost all day. I expected to find her dead under the roost any morning. But instead I began to find one egg in the nest each morning. By making several trips after roosting time I discovered how she managed.

"When it was night, and the other hens had gone to roost with their heads tucked under their wings, the last faint clucking would tell her that it was safe to move. She would make her certain way down the cleated plank to the floor of the henhouse, feed, scratch in the litter, but without the noisy clucking that usually accompanies scratching. Then she would find her way to the same laying box and lay her egg. I suppose she went back up to the roost when she heard the first stirring at dawn.

"But that's not the end of the story. Hens usually only lay well until they are three or four years old. After all the others had been sold as culls, she laid the regular laying season for two more years. I always thought it was because her blindness had forced her to adjust to a quieter and slower way of life."

"The creatures afford some lessons worth observing," added Walter Johnston.

"The whippoorwill must be the loneliest creature in the whole world," Tor said after he had waited for his grandfather to continue the adult conversation. But his grandfather had been listening to the whippoorwill, too.

"Why do you think it so lonely?" Walter Johnston asked the boy.

"Because it has said 'whip-poor-will' over and over again for two hundred and thirty-seven times. I counted them. And it sounds so lonely it sends shivers up my spine."

"And all two hundred and thirty-seven came from the same place—none farther or nearer," Walter Johnston said. "The whippoorwill does not flit around much. I've seen only one or two in my whole life. Maybe the awareness that it doesn't think it necessary to be seen and the fact that it doesn't change its song added up to make it the most unlonely creature. It's found a song that it can live with."

"I wonder what the loneliest creature is then?" Tor asked.

"It might be man," the visitor answered. "He seems to be about the only creature who can't find a song that suits him. He's always trying to change his tune."

"And right now it's already way past tune-changing time for you," Angus MacLeod said to the boy. "It's time for a dream tune in your soft bed. You can dream of herding the Black-faced Highlands in the high meadows and still wake up rested. That's the good thing about dreaming."

Tor was glad enough to say good night, for the talk of the evening had been dull and quiet, with none of Mr. Johnston's exciting stories. But once upstairs, the distant voices and the creak of the rockers on the stones below dispelled the drowsiness he had felt. So with the pillow and top quilt from his bed he crept quietly through the window and stretched himself on the porch roof to listen.

Far beyond the orchard, past the fields that ran over the eastern slope of the ridge, the whippoorwill was still pouring one lonely "whip-poor-will" after another into the mist that lay over the valley but stopped somewhere below the fields. There was no moon, but the mountain sky was thicker with stars than the day pasture with daisies in June. And skimming the fields as high as the tops of the apple trees, with a few scattered ones twinkling above the roof line of the house, the fireflies blinked their lights, playing ticktacktoe in a thousand little squares of night. Tor watched for two to collide, as he had often watched for a falling star to hit another, but neither ever did.

Below, the voices droned on with the deep talk about man being the loneliest creature. "Never satisfied, is the trouble," he heard his grandfather say, and the rockers of his chair squeaked louder on the stone.

"It's that whippoorwill," Tor said to himself. "That's what makes me feel lonely." But the mention of his name below pulled his ears back from far away.

"I worry about Tor," Angus MacLeod was saying. "He's a born land lover. He's beginning to talk of going to agricultural school and coming back to live on the land."

"But he will change," Tor heard his grandmother reply. "Our boys were off and on in their thinking while they were growing up."

Tor wondered if he would change. "What would be so bad about a highway through the land? Wouldn't it be fun to watch the lights of the cars whizzing past at night and listen to the powerful hum of the giant truck engines, grinding up the grades from ridge to ridge, making more noise than three red tractors? And I'll have a light-colored car, with a top that comes down, not black like Grandpa's. I'll whiz past Martha Hillyer's house on the way to town on Saturday afternoon and blow the horn and make the brakes squeal. And when she gets over being such a smart aleck, I'll take her with me. Her hair will blow in the wind, and I'll tell her to wear a headband the color of my car."

The voices below trailed off into faint murmurs. The rockers over the stone became rhythmic ticktack-ticks, slowing like a gate tapping its latch post in a dying breeze. The heavy vapor which hung at the edge of the mountain fields soaked up the last calls of the whippoorwill. A dampness settled on the patchwork quilt that Tor had pulled close about his chin. The people below had talked too long. Sleep had overtaken the listener before he could drag himself through the window to his soft bed.

The sleeper turned his head on the damp pillow and his body on the hard slate roof, and dreamed. A paved driveway split the lawn and ended at the east end of the porch. Instead of rocking chairs, a bright-yellow car with its top down stood on the stone floor. From the farther edge of the lawn the driveway skirted the graveyard wall and joined a wide highway which divided the fields below. At the west end of the graveyard wall another paved strip led through the orchard to the barnyard gate. A cattle truck and two smaller ones stood on the grass near the barnyard gate. The doors of each truck carried a neatly lettered inscription: SKYLAND STOCK FARM. The barnyard itself held an assortment of tractors, four in number, ranging from small to monstrous, all bright red.

A young man wearing shiny boots, a white shirt open at the neck and a fawn-colored Western Stetson hat stood with a hand on the open door of the yellow convertible, watching the cars and trucks whiz past, more going north than south. The young man was Tor MacLeod, progressive stock farmer. Now he entered the car, backed over the ancient stones, halted with a squeal of the tires at the edge of the asphalt apron, then passed the fields too fast to pay much attention to them on the way to the road. He waved to a farmhand who was climbing on one of the tractors.

The state hadn't taken the land after all. Grandpa MacLeod had been all wrong. The road had scarcely harmed the land. As a matter-of-fact, everything had worked out for the good. A lot of money had been paid for the right-of-way. All the extra money had made it possible to modernize, to buy machinery, to make progress.

The dreamer mumbled something in his sleep, "Has anyone seen Grandpa?" No one had seen Grandpa. He was nowhere to be found. The young farmer, Tor, tells a farmhand not to call or look for him anymore. The dreamer talks in his sleep again, "Wait for me, Grandpa, I want to go."

And now Tor is at the county fair. His Shorthorn bulls have won the top prizes. His Black-faced Highland sheep and his Cheviots have blue ribbons hanging on the front of their pens. The tall young farmer in his shiny boots and stetson hat gives orders to two hired men who tend the cattle and the sheep: "Groom them for the auction. I want top prices."

Now the dream changes. A boy sits on a bale of hay combing the wavy wool on his pure-white Cheviot lambs. He hates the pig-nosed Southdown lambs that Martha Hillyer has in the next pen.

The tall young man stops and looks down at the boy with his lambs. "I'll buy your lambs," the young man says. "I need a new bloodline for my flock."

"They're not for sale," the boy replies. "I live with my grandfather, and this is only my fourth year of breeding to build a flock."

"What's your name, boy?" the man in the shiny boots and stetson hat asks.

"Tor MacLeod," the boy replies. "I live atop the mountain at the Middle Fields farm. I raise Cheviots, but my grandfather raises Black-faced Highlands."

"You look familiar," the man says. "Sell me your lambs. Then you can go home and sleep in your bed instead of sleeping here on two bales of hay laid end to end and living on hotdogs for a week. No use to be sentimental about things. I used to be that way myself 'til I learned that nothing has much value until it has a sale price put on it."

Tor was glad when the stranger went away. He didn't like him very much. He hoped he wouldn't come back to pester him about selling his lambs again.

Tor kicked two bales of hay together, stretched his weary muscles on them, and pulled the horse blanket over him. It was nine o'clock, and grandmother Una MacLeod had told him not to stay up "roaming around the carnival circle until all hours of the night."

"My, you go to sleep this early?" A soft voice came from the edge of the pen. He opened his eyes and looked up into the smiling face of Martha Hillyer. "Will you give my lambs fresh water in the morning before my brother gets here? He's going home with us tonight."

Martha Hillyer was still wearing the fluffy organdy dress that had had its sleeve frayed in the cogwheel of the grindstone four years ago at Tor's birthday party. She and the dress had grown up together. "How strange," Tor thought. She'd changed a lot, though. Her pigtails with ribbons on the ends were gone. Her hair hung loosely about her shoulders, and when she looked down at Tor, it came together below her chin and framed a pretty face.

"Yes. I'll water them. I'll feed them, too. Your brother needn't hurry," Tor said as he got up from his hay pallet and stood looking over the pen at the square-headed, stump-legged Southdown lambs that he thought so ugly. "But she's awful pretty," he thought to himself as he brushed the bed wrinkles and loose hay from his clean white shirt.

"I was going on the Ferris wheel with my brother before we have to meet my father in front of the ticket gate at ten o'clock. But he's gone off somewhere."

"I went on it before dark," Tor said as he chewed on a hay stalk and shifted his weight from one boot to the other. The fingers of a hand sank deep in his dungaree pocket and felt carefully through three folded dollar bills and an assortment of change. "Enough to do the carnival circle for an hour or more," he thought.

"I'd like to go again," he said.

"Come on then," Martha Hillyer said with a nervous quick giggle as she gave his shirt sleeve a slight pull.

He cleared the pen with only one hand on the top slat for leverage. Out of the corner of his eye he kept the distance measured so he'd be sure not to brush against Martha's dress as they made their way around bales of hay, grain bags, and water pails cluttering the aisle that led from the exhibit shed toward the bright lights of the carnival circle. With each step the toes of Tor's boots raised a wave of sawdust.

At the ticket window for the Ferris wheel Tor left his change in his pocket and plunked down one of his crisp dollar bills.

"Father says it only cost a dime to ride when he was young. Now it costs a quarter. My brother's got my money."

"I wouldn't let you buy your own anyway," Tor asserted with all the indifference of a big spender as he parted the two tickets and held one out to Martha.

When the Ferris wheel stopped with Tor and Martha at the very top, Martha said, "I'm afraid." But Tor was a real daredevil and swung the seat back and forth. Martha giggled and screamed at the same time. At the edge of her soft ruffled dress Tor found her hand and squeezed it.

Beyond the neon signs and naked light bulbs of the carnival circle, over a silver ribbon that the moon made of the highway, Tor was taking Martha home in his bright-yellow convertible. He was the tall young man in the shiny boots and stetson hat. Martha Hillyer's hair streamed in the night breeze as they sped over the smooth highway along the mountaintop. She was sitting very close to Tor. Her hair was blowing in his eyes as she leaned her head gently on his shoulder.

"I love your bright-colored new car," she said.

"It's sunshine yellow," the young man replied.

Tor blinked in the sunlight. He awakened to the rolling run-on notes of a purple finch that had taken his perch in the top of the ancient maple. He had fallen asleep on the roof and now it was morning. The dew had dampened the pillow and quilt. He rubbed his eyes and stretched himself. The sun was already above the mountain. He slipped quietly through the window and put his bed in order. He washed his face and studied himself in the mirror for a long time. He hadn't changed at all, but he felt taller.

He heard movement and voices far away in the kitchen. He paused in the front hallway, stood with the door ajar, and studied the end of the porch. It would be just perfect for a driveway and parking place. He'd never tell anybody all of his terribly mixed-up dream. There were parts of it which could really make sense when the time came.

In the kitchen Walter Johnston and Angus Mac-Leod were lamenting the fact that one of the most beautiful mountains where Walter Johnston lived had been scalped and its crest leveled to make a landing strip so planes could hurry guests to a resort hotel. "Hurry! Race against time," said Walter Johnston, "so they can sit motionless on the hotel veranda for the next two weeks."

"I had the strangest dream," Tor said as he took his place at the table. He would tell his grandmother the part about the road not ruining the fields later. He liked what she had said last night about adjusting to new ways. Maybe she would help him get Grandpa to change some—road or no road. At least get some modern machinery like Mr. Hillyer's.

"You had your head too full of grown folks' talk when you went to bed," Una MacLeod volunteered. But Tor was counting the third spoonful of sugar for his oatmeal and didn't hear. He was also wondering if he would tell Martha Hillyer the part about the Ferris wheel and the yellow car.

❧ Ten ❧

"**Y**ou will find that information from your congressman or state assemblyman will be slow in coming and vague in content," Walter Johnston volunteered to Angus as they sat at breakfast. Angus had suggested that Walter not continue on his way until after mail time, as he expected official news momentarily. "And when you do hear it will only be a referral note to some official department. At least that's the way it was when they took our mountaintop for an airfield. The government appropriated money because a landing strip for hotel guests somehow became indispensable to our country's defense. So what information we got finally came from the Chief of Army Engineers. But long before we knew what was going on, they had abstracted descriptions of the land they wanted from the land records in the county courthouse.

"A smooth-talking realtor showed up at our place with a map and description of the land they wanted. He said he had a client who wanted to buy it. Of course we said it was not for sale.

"Within a week, however, we learned that others who owned land in the area had been approached to sell. Some did. Then the procedure of seizure, under the law of eminent domain, began. First, state-appointed appraisers came, not asking the value we put on our land, but rather telling us its value.

"We took our case to the appellate court, appealing to the court not to make us sell against our will. The court appointed court referees, three retired judges, to referee the argument of price, not whether we would sell. That had been determined on the drawing board in some government office long before."

"I'll take a trip to the county courthouse and see if there've been any title searchers around," Angus MacLeod said.

"Might be wise to check the counties at either end of the proposed highway. It's sort of a pincers movement, closing in with all possible speed and great quiet," Walter Johnston suggested. "They usually work from both ends. Once they start, speed means a lot to them. The element of surprise, catching people off guard, works in their favor."

Tor listened. He thought he might even tell his grandfather that he had dreamed the land wasn't taken for a national forest and that the highway came but didn't hurt the fields. But he was chewing on a thick strip of bacon. By the time he had finished chewing, Walter Johnston's description had become so grim that Tor even began to feel guilty about his dream.

"To try to resist," Mr. Johnston said, "is like trying to walk through a maze of dark corridors, always thinking a light will shine for you at the end of one. But it never does. The thread of hope that one holds onto as a guide really leads only to added confusion and despair.

"We face the grim possibility of living in a country the major part of which will be covered with asphalt or concrete. Seventy acres for an entrance-exit labyrinth is not unusual.

"What is authorized in legal terms as 'feasible and prudent' is nothing more than a confirmation of what has proved convenient to engineers and will present fewer obstacles or greater challenges (depending on the mood of the engineers) to the bulldozers.

"To keep the bonanza going for the varied industrial, commercial, construction and political interests, the concrete juggernaut pushes on. Homes, whole neighborhoods, parks, fields, forests and streams, historic sites—all disappear in its wake."

Tor and his grandfather walked almost a mile past the mailbox with their guest when he left after breakfast. Angus MacLeod pointed out the route that would take the road from Humpstack Gap to Fisher's rock and leave his fields untouched.

"Hope for the best, but remember Una's story of the blind hen," Walter Johnston said as he shook hands with Angus. He patted Tor on the shoulder and said, "Stick close to your grandfather. You two need each other." Then, turning back to Angus, he said, "Keep me informed and if I can help in any way, send for me."

Tor was looking at the half moon he was making in the dust with the toe of his boot. The picture from his dream of the highway, his sports car, the tractors in the barn lot ran before him. He felt mingled guilt and excitement. He found no words to reply to Mr. Johnston.

Walter Johnston disappeared around the bend of the road at his leisurely pace. His canvas haversack swung at his side, measuring his steps. The man and the boy stood for a long time after he was gone.

Back at the barn the morning chores were carried out in almost total silence, except for Angus MacLeod's calling favorite animals by name as he moved them about their place to stall or stanchion. When the feeding and milking chores were finished, Angus brought the two harnessed teams of workhorses from the barn to drink at the watering trough. "The corn is still dripping with dew, but we'll go to the cultivating anyway," he said. "I hope we can finish by dinner time. I want to go to the courthouse afterward and see if there's been anybody meddling in the land records."

The corn was black-green, reflecting the richness of the earth. Its top blades fanned the horses' bellies as they moved along the rows. The rubbing of the blades and an occasional swish of the tail kept horse- and deerflies from pestering the horses. Wire muzzles kept the horses from nibbling at the blades.

Except at the end of the row, where Tor pulled the digger lever back and drew the reins to turn the team carefully so they would not trample the end stalks, there was little that needed his attention. He marveled at the particular care his team took to move their great hooves in turning. They seemed to understand that no stalk was to be broken or trampled. Of course Tor had been given the older, less-spirited team, which he would not have picked if he had been given the choice. He liked the younger, prancing pair of chestnut-colored mares which his grandfather used. The monotony of the long rows, with nothing to do but sit astride the cultivator seat, holding the reins lightly and watching the corn row pass beneath him, made him drowsy. Then the vision of the big red tractor swam before his eyes, cultivating four or six rows at once, instead of two.

Every twelve or sixteen rows his grandfather called to him to let the horses rest. Then the man and boy sat together on the stone wall at the end of the field. "This will be the last cultivating," his grandfather said. "After it's belly-high, the weeds can't get much of a start. There's too much shade. If we get the right rain, we'll have a good crop." He complimented Tor on how skillfully he maneuvered the team in turning without damaging the end stalks. Tor listened and felt a little guilty. His mind kept going back to his dream—the barn lot full of tractors and a tractor with a four- or six-row cultivator attached.

The last row was finished well before dinner time. Angus MacLeod stood for a long time watching the sun polish the green waves with a silvery-green sheen as the breeze turned the underside of the blades up to it. "It's laid by," he said. "We plan, we plant, we bring it to the laying-by point, and then we leave the rest to the weather and the Almighty."

"There's time to unharness the horses before dinner," the boy said.

Some of Grandpa's talk left Tor with nothing to

do but keep quiet or change the subject. If he kept quiet, he puzzled over what Grandpa had said and found a little voice inside him saying, "Remember this. Remember what your grandfather says." If he changed the subject, it usually helped his mind get away from pestering itself.

"We'll leave the cultivators here," Angus said to the boy as he called "Whoa." The easy swinging clip-clop walk of the teams and the whispered whine of axles needing grease came to a stop at the front of the storage shed. "I'll clean and grease the working parts before I put them away for another year. Rust does more harm than use if tools aren't cared for."

Their trace chains having freed them, the horses shook their foam-flecked flanks and quickened their pace toward the watering trough. Angus MacLeod stooped by the edge of the shed and picked up two or three nondescript feathers, a matted fragment of wool, and two twigs. He pointed to the beam under the roof. Two or three twigs stuck over the edge.

"A Carolina wren's nest," he said as he pointed to the beam and held out his hand to show Tor the fragments he had gathered from the ground. "The wind could pile a leaf, a stem and a feather or two with more care. Beside the yellow-billed cuckoo, the Carolina wren builds the shoddiest nest of any bird that lays its eggs above ground level. It was building in April when I took the corn planter out. Now it's raised the young and they've flown away. I didn't show it to you then. I thought you might get too curious, come to look too often, and cause her to desert."

"What held the nest together while the young were growing up?" Tor asked and quickly added, "I know better'n to go peering too close or touching a bird's nest with eggs or baby birds in it."

"Faith held it together, I guess," Angus replied. "Faith is like a skein of string we keep wound about our hearts like thread on a spool. We keep unwinding it, and it never runs out. But if we let it get all tangled up so that it won't unwind anymore, everything falls apart."

"I'll bring the horses in," Tor said as he moved away. If he listened to Grandpa go on, his mind would get away from thinking about the swimming hole where he was planning to go after dinner and stay until time to bring the cows.

"It's even worse if it's wound too tight and breaks," his grandfather's voice trailed after him as the boy moved across the lot to bring the horses to the barn.

After dinner Angus got ready to go to the courthouse. He asked Tor if he would like to go. "It's too hot in town," the boy said. "All I could do would be buy an ice-cream cone at Fletcher's Drugstore, and then sit on the wall in front of the courthouse and wait. I don't like the inside of the courthouse, too dark and musty. I think I'll go to the swimming hole 'til cow time or ride my bike down and swim with David Hillyer."

"If you do, leave Shep at home; it's too hot for him to run panting after your bicycle. I'll let the horses out. You bring the cows if I'm late."

"I'll let the horses out. I like to watch them roll in the grass to get the dried sweat off," the boy said.

"You had better take your reading glasses," Una MacLeod reminded Angus.

After his grandfather left, Tor turned the horses out to pasture. He leaned over the gate and watched as each horse found its own bare spot in the grass and rolled from side to side, treading air with its feet. Dust rose as they tossed their manes and shook themselves. The boy watched as they ambled toward the shade of the largest tree along the fence line, snipping off the bloom of Queen Anne's lace as they went. The boy patted Shep on the head and spoke to him. "We'll go swimming. But let's go back and talk to Grandmother first."

"I thought you'd be halfway to the swimming hole by now," Una MacLeod said to the boy as she looked at him over the top of the newspaper she had just settled in her rocker to read.

"I wanted to ask you something first. Why is Grandpa so worried? Do you think he'll find out that they're really going to build a highway up here?"

"He feels it stronger now than he ever has before. He has a way of feeling what's going to be."

"But what would be so bad about it? I dreamed about it last night and saw the road in my dream. It didn't seem to hurt the fields at all."

"I think what worries him most is the idea of taking all the land the way they did from Bent Mountain to Thornton's Gap. He has loved it so long. To have that happen would be hard to bear."

"I felt guilty all morning because I had liked the highway in my dreams. I wouldn't dare tell Grandpa."

"But whatever happens, we'll adjust. The fields he has loved will be a part of him forever."

"I think me and Shep will go to the swimming hole until time to bring the cows."

"Shep and I, please. Your mother and Dr. Charlton will be here in a few days, so polish up your grammar. And take a cake of soap with you to get that cornland from behind your ears and under your chin so you won't leave a row of earth thick enough to plow around the bathtub. And have fun. One day you'll need the swimming hole for a memory. Don't worry about dreams that disagree with your grandpa's feelings."

The swimming hole was at the southern edge of the second field that had already been cleaned of its hay crop and whose new grass was just beginning to give the brown stubble a tint of green. The mountain springs high up at the base of Hanging Gardens formed one stream; the spring that came from under the wall of the field, which had been made from a swamp, formed another. They came together at the swimming hole, and their current formed a whirlpool which went around and around, not allowing silt to settle before it cascaded over the saw-toothed limestone below. The current had cut away at the mossy banks, but the twisted and gnarled roots of tall sycamores on one side and limestone projections on the other had kept it in bounds. Where the sunlight came through the branches of the sycamore trees and shone on the water, Tor could see the slanting ledge which formed the bottom.

Shep picked his way over the stones where the

stream poured into the pool. He paddled aimlessly with the current one full circle and sprayed his half-undressed master as he climbed the bank and shook himself. Then with a hurt look in his eyes, from the scolding he received, he stretched himself full length, facing the boy.

"I forgive you. You're a good dog," Tor said as he eased himself down the bank over the giant roots into the cold mountain water. The dog tapped his wet tail three times against the green carpet of moss and closed his eyes to dream of driving thirsty flocks and herds to sparkling water holes.

Tor did three almost effortless turns around the outer edge of the pool with the current. He stood neck-deep in the middle of the sun-flecked water and used the soap as his grandmother had directed. He wondered why using soap in a bathtub was so aggravating but in a swimming hole was almost fun.

Stretched close to Shep on the moist green carpet, Tor let the town, Fletcher's Drugstore, and the ice-cream cone he would have had, flick once across his mind. He studied the midsummer sky. It was moving far away. In April it was so close its clouds rolled like wool sacks against the hilltops. Now the faraway mare's tail clouds drifted higher and higher to nothingness. "A dry sky, Grandpa would say," the boy whispered to the sleeping dog.

With a hollow elderberry stalk, which he kept at the base of the nearest sycamore, he tried to get a soap bubble up to the leaves of the lowest branches of the giant trees, but more than a hundred years of reaching for the sun had stretched them up and up too far.

From somewhere above the swimming hole a crayfish had dug an underground sluiceway to lay her eggs in some damp gravel bed. The stream had worked its way through the maze of roots and dropped as a tiny waterfall over the edge of the bank. Tor wondered if it would take it a hundred or a thousand years to erode the bank back and back until a stream the size of his little finger felled a sycamore which his arms could not reach one-fourth of the way around.

The high-pitched "che-wink, che-wink" of a towhee came to him from the edge of the woods. "Summer is over the hump and on the wane when the towhees come from the deep woods and start working the edge," Tor had learned from his grandfather. The forlorn call of a dove added loneliness to the other sounds of summer. Maybe he would go and swim with David Hillyer.

He watched a monarch butterfly drive a dainty cherry-spotted one from a milkweed blossom. He studied a chipmunk, that wise little animal that gets his work done in spring and early summer, then slows his pace through the hot months, amble along a twisted root and disappear under it. If he went swimming with Dave Hillyer, he would tell him not to throw stones at Martha and make her go back home. He scolded the monarch under his breath. Bees worked up and down the spires of Morden's pink, where it contested with milkweed for standing space along the banks of the stream. He broke a spike of Morden's pink and held it under his nose. Its delicate fragrance blended with the sweet smell of milkweed, which came to him on the air from twenty feet away.

Tor closed his eyes against the sun's rays that found little holes between the arched roof of broad sycamore leaves and poured down on him like shafts of golden rain. When the sprig of pink dropped from his hand, it made no sound. But something stirred the sleeping dog. Shep raised himself on his front paws and surveyed all points of the compass around his master. At intervals he rose and walked a wide circle around the boy. When the sun had fallen low enough, the dog came and stood over him. Shep wagged his tail and whined. It was time to bring home the cows.

❧ Eleven ❧

Angus MacLeod was already at the barn when Tor arrived with the cows. The boy studied the movements of the man. There was no "sign of aggravation," as Una MacLeod called it, when his grandfather was disturbed about something. When work was finished, the man leaned with his elbows over the night pasture gate. The boy climbed up two slats so his elbows could rest on the top and make a brace for his chin.

The man looked across the cornland, waxy-green, to the pasture beyond where the sleek Shorthorns were grazing, their red coats almost aglow where the low sun was striking their flanks. His eye scanned the farthest green where Black-faced Highland sheep, scarcely more than specks, moved with the slow contentment of creatures well fed. The farm bell broke the silence, announcing suppertime.

"What did you find out in town?" Tor asked. He had tried to wait for Angus to speak first, but the suspense was too much.

"I'll tell you and your grandmother at supper. I got back just in time for chores and haven't had a chance to tell her either."

When the three were seated at the supper table, Angus began as he had promised. "Mother, I guess you're right about my staying too close to the mountain. If I'd got out more, I would have known what's been going on. It's too bad Walter left this morning. Almost everything he said has already been going on. All the deeds and records were abstracted two years ago, before those people went through here surveying. The lady in the Records Office said the original plan called for the road to go all the way to Eagle's Aerie. That it was the war that stopped it at Thornton's Gap. That we had, of course, heard before the war. She said the money has already been appropriated and that the whole thing is supposed to go ahead now as originally planned and be completed in two or three years."

"And the government will take the land, too?" Tor broke in.

"Let your grandfather finish," Tor's grandmother spoke quietly and added not so quietly, "You did a good job with your neck and ears, but there's enough plow dirt under your fingernails to start a seedbed."

"I also learned at the courthouse that Ernest Adair has been made the local appraiser for the land in our county. He'll work with two outsiders."

"All the land on the mountain?" Una asked, taking up Tor's question.

"The whole crown of the mountain, several miles wide, just like the part that comes to Thornton's Gap, a scenic highway and campsites in national forestland. I went to the bank to see Adair.

He had a government bulletin and map called U.S. Scenic Highways and National Forests. It shows what's been completed, what's in progress, and what's in the planning stage. It shows ours in progress, the whole wide strip colored in light green as national forest and the road in double black lines all the way. It misses Hillyer's farm. Takes in Adair's and the two farms he has bought. I didn't get too good a look at the map. He said he got it from the State Highway Engineer in his capacity as condemnation appraiser; wasn't supposed to let it out. He made me hopping mad. Said he'd been driving up and down the mountain all these years. Was glad something was happening to move him off. Said as we get older, we're better off in the valley where it's a little easier living."

"I hope you didn't show your temper," Una MacLeod said softly.

"No, I didn't. When he said that, I was already leaving. As I left, he said, 'You'll get a good price, Angus.' I said, 'We'll see.' And that was all."

The softness of his grandfather's voice mystified Tor. Was he too deeply disturbed to be aggravated? Tor wondered. Was there nothing left to fight and stand up for? Grandpa could stand up against anything. The soft voice of his grandfather stirred up a feeling that something terrible was happening before his very eyes, but Tor could not see it. But worse yet, it made no sound. Tor wished Grandpa would stomp his foot or scrape his chair on the floor as he did when he was angry.

Angus MacLeod had finished his supper. He pushed back his chair without a sound. Tor looked at his grandmother. She had folded her napkin. Half her food was still on her plate. Part of the first helpings were still on his own.

"Why, you aren't eating," his grandmother said. "Swallowed too much water at the swimming hole, I guess."

"I guess. I'll scrape the plates for Shep."

"I'll get out of the way," the man said as he moved toward the door. "I'll be on the porch."

Tor came back from feeding his dog to wipe the dishes without being called. "Grandpa doesn't seem upset," he said to his grandmother when he knew Angus was out of hearing.

"He's thinking," Una answered the boy.

When the kitchen was straight and Tor and Una went to the porch, Angus didn't ask what was in the paper as he always did in summer when he was too tired to read it or just didn't want to take the time from gazing out upon his world. He took up where he had left off at the table.

"When I left Adair's bank, I went back to the courthouse and asked some more questions. I found out they've already bought or condemned the north and south ends—Madison and Nelson counties. 'But there are enough people left to stop it,' I said to myself.

"So I went to Judge Garber's office and had him write up a petition opposing both national forest and highway. There's nothing legal about it, but I wanted it on legal paper and typewritten. That's why I went to the judge.

"He was very nice about it but felt that I would be wasting my time. I told him that the last crop was just laid by this morning; that between now and harvest I could find out how others felt about having their lives uprooted and thrown to the wind like chaff.

"He said he comes up to the mountain, like Moses, when he is pondering important decisions; said it widened his perspective. Paid our place a great compliment. Said our fields didn't look tilled; said they looked sculptured, like some mighty giant had chiseled away at the mountaintop until he had a checkerboard design of smooth meadows. I told him if the Creator hadn't wanted the land used and tended, He wouldn't have given man brains enough to make a spade."

"What'll you do with the petition after it's signed?" Tor's grandmother asked.

"Send one to the governor and a copy to my congressman. When I told them at the courthouse I hadn't heard anything from my letters, they said they'd probably be referred to the State Highway Engineer and the Federal Highway Commissioner. Said it was a little late to expect much. I said, 'It's never too late until they send the sheriff to drive me off by force, and the bulldozers are ripping the guts out of my land.'"

Tor straightened up in his chair. Now Grandpa was being his real self. But why didn't he raise his voice? He spoke as though someone who shouldn't hear might be listening behind the thick log walls or beyond the edge of the porch.

"Would they destroy the house, too?" the boy asked. And as he asked the question, it came to him. The man was speaking softly because he felt the fields and buildings, the old half maple tree in the yard, and the stone walls of the burying ground would hear.

Night sounds and the tinkle of sheep bells behind the stone walls came in to fill the long pause in the man's talk. The boy was crying, but that, too, he did softly, deep down inside, without even having to disguise a sob with a clipped cough or a pretended nose blow.

The man did not answer the boy's question. "If the petition fails," he continued, "I'll have the state and federal engineers here and convince them that the only sensible place for a road is west —from Humpstack Gap to Fisher's Rock—and that this section, with the Indian mounds and all, should not be touched. If that fails, I'll go to court to save my rights and get justice. A batter has three strikes before he's out."

"It's past your bedtime, Tor," the woman said.

"And tomorrow we'll start visiting some farms to get signers," Angus said. "I'm glad we've got a few weeks' lull before second haying and corn harvest."

Tor said good night and went up the stairs in the dark. The stairs creaked in the heavy quiet.

He did not crawl out on the roof to listen. He was still crying, but now he could blow his nose and no one would hear him.

The tinkle of the bells moved far away. He complained in his sleep. His dream was not of big red tractors and blue ribbons for prize animals at the fair. The barn was falling down, and the fields were caving in like the ones in earthquake pictures in his geography book.

If the boy had crawled out on the roof to listen, he would have heard the man continuing to speak softly, without waver or qualification, of his determination to keep his own beautiful world which endless years and generations of toil and care had shaped. He would also have heard the quiet approval of the gentle woman confirming a faith that the man speaking could indeed move mountains.

If Angus MacLeod's contented isolation had caused him to be one of the last to learn what was going on, he now set about to make up the lost time with all possible speed.

"I'm going to start with my petition today," he said at breakfast. "I'll go north one day and south the next and work from the far ends toward the middle."

"Can I go with you?" Tor asked.

"If you don't get restless while I'm visiting with the people. You'll tire of it in a day or two."

Only in a few places were there roads which led along the mountain from one farm to another, so day after day and week after week, Angus Mac-Leod went down the mountain and took the valley pike north or south to the roads which led back up to the mountain farms.

Tor's grandfather was right. After a few days Tor chose to stay at home, not really for the reasons his grandpa thought. He hated to see his grandfather disappointed.

In many places "a nice man" from the government had already been there with a paper to sign. Those who didn't sign had either received, or were expecting, appraisers to negotiate a price. Some laughed at the futility of Angus' effort, some sympathized; few were willing to fight.

The reasons given for their actions were as many as the people themselves. One tall, solemn mountain woman, who had never married, was going to use the money to buy a house in the valley "with a wide, straight staircase." The stairs in her present house were so crooked and narrow that when her father died upstairs, his body had to be let down in a sheet from a window. His foxhounds had missed him so much while he was sick that "they bounced and whelped around the corpse so much that the neighbors could hardly get it away to be laid out in the front room." She didn't want that to happen to her.

Angus learned quickly to predict the nature of the response from the general appearance of a place. If the fields were clean, the buildings in good repair, the dooryard free of weeds and the house reflecting the pride of the owner, he usually got a signer, though almost never an expression of much hope.

A barnyard full of machinery, an overgrown lot with three or four abandoned cars, a barn roof patched with tar paper usually brought the response: "I'm glad to get away from this place. I've broken my back trying to make a living on this mountain for twenty-five, thirty, forty years, and I've been in debt the whole time. Now I'll be outa debt for the first time in my life, and I can't do any worse somewhere else. No. I'm ready to sell."

"Why I wanta move to the valley?" said grizzled Newt Warren, through his tobacco-stained week's growth of chin stubble. "I hear the coon huntin's better down there. The coons have moved to the valley. I hear they're even plentiful in the town. Pickin' up here has even got so bad the coons had to leave. I'll follow 'em."

Newt Warren's barn leaned heavily to the south, half its siding gone from the east end, and a black sheet of plastic stretched over the rafters where the tin had blown off in a storm three years before. One of Newt's complaints was that he had to replace the plastic several times a year. Angus thought to ask why he didn't use tin and make it permanent, but did not. For one thing it was hard to talk to Newt. A dozen coon hounds penned in the bottom of a silo, the top half of which was gone, shook the mountain with their chorus as long as a stranger was on the place.

Cyrus McCue's place had been in his family almost as long as Angus MacLeod's. But Cyrus had married a girl from one of the valley towns who had spent only the first six years of their married life on the mountain. Then she demanded to live down in town.

Cyrus McCue kept a clean farm. He had a hired man and his family on the place. His own house was well kept, but it breathed loneliness.

"About the time the first child reached school age," Cyrus said, "I had to get a house in town. So for the past twenty-eight years I've lived up and down. My children grew up not knowing where to call home. But she would never come back to the mountain. Pampered the children to make them favor her. The boys used to come up with me some in the summer. Then it got so they only came when they'd wrecked cars and needed money. I'd give in rather than get a tongue-lashing from her. The children haven't turned out very well. They could have had all this." He swung his arms in a circle to take in the land. "Now if the government takes the place, they'll peck away at the money like buzzards after a carcass until it's all gone. Who knows what'll happen to me?"

"The proud man who had failed because of circumstances," as Angus described him to Una when he came home, like others, signed but showed little hope.

The summer was over. The corn had been cut and stood in rows of shocks which followed the contour of the sculptured land. Sumac and dogwoods were aflame along the roadsides when Angus MacLeod made a second visit to several people who had not signed but "wanted time to think about it."

Meanwhile he had received letters from his county assemblyman and congressman. Each had referred him to proper agencies for further information. The congressman had, however, written that "least productive land is naturally desirable for park and forest reservation." Angus wrote a scathing answer describing what the MacLeod farm had produced over the years, challenging him to come and see for himself "the havoc about to be done and the lives uprooted."

But Angus did not send the letter. His petition contained fewer than half the names of the mountain landowners. For those who hadn't signed, the land had not been productive. "But it was not the *land's* fault," he said to Una MacLeod when Tor was not around to hear.

Tor looked for a change in his grandfather's contentment and security which was a part of autumn's gathering in, but he found none. The measure mark of crops was put on the bins, and the year marked down as usual.

Tor collected his summer wages in Shorthorn calves, so now he had the beginning of his own herd. He groomed and curled their sleek coats daily after Grandpa had said, "We'll enter them at the fair; they'll win the spring calf prize. And next year when you have more lambs to get four or six the same size, we'll win with them."

At the fair he won second prize for the best spring calves. He bought cotton candy with Dave and Martha Hillyer, but everybody paid for his own. He'd walked back to the sheep pavilion with them and let Martha's lambs lick at his cotton candy when he tired of it. It got the wool on their noses all smudged and sticky. Martha had to work on them with soap and water. She'd been awful mad. But she got over it pretty fast.

When school started that year, she didn't pester him on the school bus anymore. Once when she was carrying a cardboard map that she'd won as a prize in history class, with her hands already full of books and a lunch pail, Tor carried her lunch pail so she would have a free hand for the map. That was the first time he sat in the same seat with her on the bus. He'd thought about it before. After that first time it was easy. He sat with her almost every day.

When she had an assignment in science class to

gather autumn leaves from all the different trees that grew on the mountain, she asked Tor to help her. He had learned them all from his grandfather. So she sent her books and lunch pail home with her brother, David. Tor put his in the mailbox, and he and Shep walked all the way home with her, gathering leaves of all kinds and colors.

Tor didn't get back home until dusk was gathering. All the chores were finished.

"I saw you from the kitchen window; otherwise we would have been worried," his grandmother said.

During supper he took a lot of teasing from his grandfather, but he felt too good to let it rattle him. On the way back up the mountain from Martha Hillyer's house the glow of the mellow lowering autumn sun had given the boy's heart a warm mysterious glow which he had never felt before, and he had whispered his secret to Shep.

"Except for a very few," Angus MacLeod said to Tor one bright October day as they leaned over the barnyard gate when chores were finished, "all the people who didn't sign the petition wanted money for debts or something. If they thought they could get a good price for rights-of-way for a highway and keep their property, they'd all sign. Next week I'm going to put a new roof on the blacksmith shop, and then before snow flies, I'll have every name on a new petition."

Tor started to ask why, with things so uncertain, Grandpa didn't wait about the roof, but he kept quiet, listening to the certainty in the voice of the man who continued, "At the same time I'll start working on the highway engineer to get him up here and show him how sensible it would be to put the road from Humpstack Gap to Fisher's Rock and bypass us."

Just beyond the barnyard a meadowlark began to add the mellowness of song to the golden softness of the autumn trees in the lowering sun.

"The larks will be moving in for the winter," the man said. "And it's about time we took old Blue Boy and Tennessee Belle to the high pasture and the Hanging Gardens to start a fox."

When the new roof was finished, Angus went to Judge Garber to get help in drawing up a new petition. He came home with much to tell.

"The judge has changed his mind," Angus began at the supper table. "He said that 'one man in the right is a majority,' and it looks like I might just be that man. He read me about three examples where people fought cases something like ours and won.

"The best one was about a man in Ames, Iowa, and a hundred-year-old cottonwood tree. Now, a cottonwood tree isn't good for much but shade, but this man thought that it didn't have to be cut down to make way for a road. He fought it and won. They moved the road and left the tree.

"And in Moundsville, a few people in Ohio and West Virginia stopped a highway from going through Indian mound country. They battled it through the courts and won.

"In North Carolina, the people in the Big Santeetlah Valley kept a highway out. Judge Garber thinks the best we can hope for is to save the land; thinks it's gone too far to stop the road."

Tor heard Judge Garber's last remark and felt a

mixture of pleasure and guilt. His dream picture of a modern stock farm came back, as it often did. But dreaming in opposition to his grandfather made him feel guilty.

The urgency of the fight to save his world cried "Hurry!" for Angus MacLeod. But autumn was an important part of his world. Autumn was the time for a man to slow down after the explosive growth of summer. In summer a man almost had to run or miss the next burst of bloom or ripening harvest. Autumn for Angus MacLeod was a time to look back and be thankful, to stand and listen to the faint, faraway gabble of wild geese, search the sky for their mile-high V penciled against the sky, and watch until it vanished.

He found time to listen to a barred owl in the twilight and sit high in his meadows with Tor, listening to old Blue Boy and Tennessee Belle give added harmony to the rhythm of a moon-drenched night.

He carried his petition back to the mountain landowners. Before short-dayed November was half gone, he had every name except three: Newt Warren, the woman who wanted a house with a wide, straight staircase, and Cyrus McCue. Cyrus had hanged himself from a barn beam with the hayfork rope.

❧ Twelve ❧

Angus MacLeod spent most of the winter mailing his petition to one official or agency after another. He watched for the mailman from the kitchen window. Una MacLeod watched as he stood in the winter's wind or storm reading by the mailbox when a reply came, not waiting to sit before the fireplace as he had always done. Impatience was replacing a gentle patience that had set the gait and movement of the man. She responded with whatever words of encouragement she could when he came to her in the kitchen with an unfolded letter and the petition, now showing signs of frayed edges and torn folds.

The replies were all variations on the same theme which came from the Federal Highway Commissioner: "We have made a sincere and conscientious effort to situate, design, and construct a highway that will blend with the landscape. The preservation of the landscape will be assured by the acquisition of land contingent to the highway and designated a national forest.

"Environmental values and natural beauty will be preserved. Recreational areas are planned which will afford many citizens opportunities that will enhance their appreciation of the beauty of our nation.

"The recommendation proposed in your petition would curtail the opportunities of the many and give favor to an extremely limited few. These few will, of course, enjoy full compensation under the best value judgment available and the due process of law."

At the height of winter, when the wind blew hardest and the snow-crusted fields seemed lifeless, the dreaded agents came to catch the unsuspecting when they thought the land dwellers would most readily comply.

First came an agent with papers to be signed, giving the government the right to buy at a price agreed on by owner and appraisers. "But my land is not for sale," Angus MacLeod replied after the man had made idle conversation and sheepishly arrived finally at the purpose of his visit. "And if something is not for sale, it has no price to be arrived at. No, I'm sorry for your long trip up, but I'll never sign away my land."

Una MacLeod's fears were unfounded, for she had dreaded an explosion of anger. But Angus spoke softly, and stirred the fire to warm his guest.

"And what would you consider a fair price for your farm?" one of the two strangers who came with Ernest Adair asked a few days after the first agent's visit.

And Angus repeated, "If something is not for sale, it has no price."

"But this is all legal," the stranger said.

"But sometimes the law overlooks a man's

heart," Angus answered. "If it's legal for the government to send people measuring and driving pegs over my land, lying about why they are here, then, with all decisions made, pretend to seek agreement with the victims, then I say the law allows for stealing."

"A grant of eminent domain gives the right to go on private property," one of the strangers volunteered.

Tor understood the disappointments which his grandmother spoke quietly to him about as they came to his grandfather. "Will I have to go back to the city to live, where there's nothing to do?" he often asked himself, never speaking it aloud to let his grandfather know that he, too, was losing hope. Sometimes he felt guilty when he thought how exciting it would be to see all kinds of big machinery moving giant stones and dynamite blasting the big cliffs at Hanging Gardens.

Sometimes his grandfather stood in the barn door looking out over the land, explaining to the boy what a letter that had come in the mail meant, or what Judge Garber had said on Angus' last visit to the courthouse. Sometimes he would change the subject and, pointing to the near fields, speak of "the crops for this year."

Tor felt proud and important when Angus took time to explain the meaning of legal terms which he brought from his visits with Judge Garber: "The process of eminent domain is the right of a government, county, state, or nation to buy a person's property against his wishes if it is considered to be in the interest of the general public. Injunction is the name of an order from the court not to do something until whoever wants to do the particular thing proves that it will harm no one or that the way chosen is the most equitable way. Equitable means just—justice."

As the winter passed, Tor learned all the terms and heard them many times.

The tall mountain man spent many of the short winter days going back for yet a third visit to the mountain landowners. When all officials with power to change, or recommend change, had refused even to make further study of the program or look over it, as both the State Highway Engineer and Federal Highway Commissioner admitted in letters they had not, Angus had gone to his friend Judge Garber for yet another petition —this one to request the court of common pleas to issue an injunction until the alternate plan of road, but no national forest, could be studied.

Bleak winter days were made colder and darker by a total absence of hope or the presence of a chilly mockery as Angus MacLeod appeared at one farmhouse after another with yet another paper begging for signers. "I was taught to stay away from lawsuits," he heard this excuse for not signing, and others, "Take a case to court over a foot of ground and you'll lose an acre." "Not me, there's too much politics. Do you think a judge would go against the bigwigs in power?" "Like there being two kinds of justice, one for the poor and one for the rich; there's two other kinds, one for the politicians and another for the rest of the people."

And the mockery: "If you keep coming back, old man, you'll be able to tear right along the top of the mountain on the new road. See that smoke risin' in the north? They're cutting and burning a swath of trees a quarter mile wide. My boy's working for them. Work that can be done in winter when the ground's froze. The same thing's happenin' to the south. I signed the government paper three months ago. There won't be a shack left on this mountain in two years."

"I wouldn't go it alone," Judge Garber said to Angus one bright March day when the judge stopped on one of his first drives of spring up the mountain. Dogwood and redbud marked the edges of the MacLeod fields. The two men stood together and watched as new lambs jumped at the side of their mothers as they went from swale to swale, finding earth's new green bursting from the unlocked crust of winter.

A few weeks later the determined mountain man was in the judge's office. "Even if I don't win, I'll feel better knowing that I made them look at my land before they destroyed it and brought the roof down from over my head," Angus MacLeod said as he put one lone signature to a plea for an injunction against the "person or persons herein named to perform and report on the alternate plan herein described not later than one hundred and eighty days from this date."

"I'll have to disqualify myself," the judge said after the two men had gone over the wording. "But Judge Holt is a good man and he is usually appointed to the court of common pleas for my district when I don't sit."

The man folded his copy of the paper and put it in his Mackinaw pocket.

"Where are you parked?" the judge asked.

"In the old livery stable lot." Angus had known it half his life as the livery stable lot. He was about to call it what everyone else did, the municipal parking lot.

"Wait. I'm through for the day and that's on my way. I'll walk with you."

On the way to the parking lot the judge mentioned the good price that the appraisers had put on Angus' farm. The man did not take up the subject. Instead he said, "We're having a good lamb crop this year. That boy Tor beats all; nearly every one of his Cheviots has had twins. He's already talking about fair time. I'm planting more than usual this year. They think mountain land don't produce. They'll see when they come, if they wait until summer."

At the entrance to the parking lot the judge stopped. "This used to be filled with horses on court days when I was a young lawyer. My! How times change. And we have to change with them, I guess."

"Too much!" the man replied as he stuck out his hand to the judge. "I wonder."

And the judge walked slowly home. He took in the daffodils and bleeding heart lining the white picket fences of his neighbors. He, too, was wondering.

Not until the crops had been laid by and more than half the hundred and eighty days had passed did the man say, "They should have been here by now."

Was it the busy days of summer which brought

the seemingly contented waiting to the man whose boldness of conviction had never made him one to tolerate delay? Was it patience taught by one disappointment after another? Or was it a hope that was slowly dying? The boy studied the man and wondered.

"I'm putting my lambs in the fair this year, too," Tor said to Martha Hillyer one day as they walked back from her swimming hole.

With the crops laid by, Tor found more and more time to go down to the Hillyers'. Martha had also made a successful stand against David so that now she badgered him. Tor and Martha walked together a lot, leaving David behind. She even rode with Tor sometimes when he drove one of her father's tractors. And once or twice they rummaged through the Hillyers' old McLean house looking at relics that had been left behind when the Hillyers had moved into their new house.

"Maybe I'll get a pen at the fair next to yours," Tor half mumbled, chewing on a blade of grass as he walked far off the path beside Martha.

"If you go early the sign-in day, unless they put different breeds together." Martha pulled at a black-eyed Susan, but the tough, spiney stem did not snap off.

"Ouch!"

"I'll get it," Tor said as he opened his pocket-knife. He gathered several and rubbed the stems against his tough palms before he gave them to Martha. She had made no critical remarks about "mouse-faced Cheviot sheep with their spindle legs," as she used to. Tor was very happy.

"I might be a lawyer if my grandfather has to give up the farm. I'm learning a lot about the law listening to him." There were several things he had wanted to say to Martha all summer, and this was one of them. "I wouldn't live in town, though. I'd live somewhere in the country like Mr. Adair, the president of the bank does, and have a farm, too, the way he has."

"That's good. I don't know what I'd like to be. A teacher maybe. There aren't many things a girl can be and live in the country. But my father says you're right smart for a boy your age. Says it's probably because you've always lived with older people. But then he said you see things more like they *are* than your grandfather. Don't you ever tell him I told you."

"When'd he say that?"

"Earlier this summer. When you asked him if you could come and work here and spend the summers, if your grandfather lost his farm. And you told him how you dreaded going back to the city to live if you had nothing to look forward to."

"He said I could. And earn wages, too. He even said I could keep my sheep and Shorthorns at the old farm if I'd help patch up the barn."

"What'd you expect, silly? That he'd make you work for nothing?"

They walked across the field together, Martha swinging a half dozen black-eyed Susans in her hand.

Word drifted along the mountain that the great earthmovers were already grading north from

Eagle's Aerie and south from Thornton's Gap. It was harvesttime and grooming time for the fair stock. One night after supper Angus MacLeod took down the calendar from the kitchen wall and leafed through the months. The hundred and eighty days were long past.

"I must go to town and find out from Judge Garber if he's heard anything," he said as he hung the calendar back in place.

"Things always move slow in court," Una MacLeod replied as she went about her work. "Maybe it'd be better not to stir them up."

Before Angus found time to go to town, the sheriff came up from town to him. He left a paper which Angus sat on the porch pondering for a long time.

"What did the sheriff bring?" Tor asked when he had waited as long as he could.

"A writ of mandamus," the man said slowly and softly.

"What's that?" the boy asked.

"It's just the opposite of an injunction. An injunction is a court order not to do something, as you already know. A writ of mandamus is an order to do something. The Federal Highway Commissioner has taken my case to the court of appeals and entered a counter-case. It's all very complicated, but what it means is I have to appear in the November term of court to show why I haven't complied with the regulations provided in the law for acquisition of property by the process of eminent domain. You know what that is."

"It's awful complicated. That'll be after the fair.

Will I still be able to take my lambs and Short-horn yearlings?"

"You'll take them," the man said, "and next year too."

Angus MacLeod wrote to his friend Walter Johnston: "I wish you would come and speak for me in court. I'd rather have you than a lawyer. It'll be before a panel of three judges, so I think we still have a good chance." Unlike the many letters which Angus had written over the past two years, an answer came back immediately: "I'll be there. But November is still a long way off. Lots could happen before then."

Angus carried his court order to Judge Garber's office. It was all news to the judge. He had heard nothing. He read the paper carefully. "I'm tempted to resign my office and take your case," he said after a long pause, when he had finished reading.

"You've done enough already."

"I wish I could speak to the judges on the panel, but that might only cause us both trouble." The judge walked down the long courthouse corridor with the man. The ancient floors squeaked under the tread of Angus' heavy boots. The judge stood watching until the man had crossed the courthouse square and disappeared out of sight around the corner past Fletcher's Drugstore.

Outwardly the harvesting followed its regular pattern. Tor watched carefully to see if Angus would make the measure mark on the corncrib and feed bins and write the year. He did. But the uncertainty of the future began to take the form of questions.

"Will you buy another farm?" Una MacLeod asked one night after Tor had gone to bed.

"No." The man answered after a long time. "We're getting along in years. Besides, I'd never feel right about it. My heart wouldn't have the proper feeling for any other land."

At the fair, Tor and Martha got their adjoining lamb pens. Tor carried water from the aisle faucet for both pens.

"Will you really leave your sheep at the old farm for my father to take care of if your grandfather has to sell his farm?" Martha asked. They talked across the pen partition, each grooming the fat lambs that made hearing difficult because of their nervous bleating. "I would help him take care of them for you until you came in the summer," Martha added as she looked away.

"But I'll sell a few. There's something I want to buy. A picture, from Mr. Benson, the artist. Then I'll leave the rest with you. I'll give them to you if you'll raise Cheviots instead of Southdowns. Their short legs make them look like pigs."

"You shut up, Tor MacLeod! I hope you don't win a single prize." But Martha was only teasing, and she knew Tor was teasing too.

It was his happiest week. He spent most of the week at the fair. He slept on his hay pallet, a little embarrassed at using the two downy comforts his grandmother had insisted that he take. An army blanket would have looked more rugged. He ate at the hotdog stands and bathed in the shower room at the end of the pavilion with total strangers. Angus and his grandmother came on judging days and brought him a change of clothes. Fair week was only five days and Martha Hillyer did not come in on one of those, but for Tor these few days were like a whole lifetime.

It was during this week that he realized a change in his way of thinking. He had been a boy wondering, sometimes puzzled and confused, about how long one had to be a boy, trying at every chance possible to act like a man.

Lying stretched out in the dark, with his stomach growling, from "eating too much junk," as his grandmother would say, amid the animal smells mixed with sawdust and hay, and the distant sounds of carnival music coming in to mix with the heavy breathing of sleeping animals, he felt his mind turn over.

Now he was a boy thinking not backward of the long time one has to be a boy, but ahead to the whole future of being a man. "Being" was the secret word. No more confusion about acting like a man or becoming one. It was being. He had stood naked in the shower stalls with other men. He had slept at one end of the sheep pavilion with no one else near. He had thought of what he would do if the place caught on fire. He had spent four dollars on carnival rides and throwing baseballs at milk bottles with Martha Hillyer. He still had six dollars in his pocket.

Part of his dream on the porch roof so long ago had already come true. It was now. And with one last exciting day of the fair still left, he lay on the hay, which smelled of June, and gazed at the rafters in the dim light that came from the one naked bulb left burning at the entrance of the pavilion.

He added to his dream. Not even the fact that his lambs had won no prizes could cast a shadow over his bright day. Besides, his yearling Shorthorns had won blue ribbons in the dual-purpose cattle class.

By midafternoon the last day of the fair Tor had helped his grandfather load the fair stock for the ride back up the mountain. Martha's father had also emptied their pens. With no more water to carry, no more grooming to do, the boy and girl did the whole dusty carnival circle again.

"It's half past nine," Martha reminded Tor as they found their way out of the Hall of Mirrors, where Martha had lost her way and screamed and Tor had held her warm hand and led her to safety, "and we have to meet my parents at the entrance gate at ten."

"Let's have one last ride on the Ferris wheel. Then we can look down on everything we've done the whole week," Tor said as he took her by the shoulder and turned her gently in the right direction.

At the top of the wheel the boy looked far out beyond the blur of lights. The harsh neon signs and naked light bulbs softened, changed, moved. They became a thousand stars. The harsh tune that kept time for the rearing ponies on the merry-go-round mellowed, and the stars seemed to dance to it. At the edge of a soft ruffle Tor found Martha Hillyer's hand. He squeezed it ever so gently—not even tight enough to hamper the night breeze from passing through fingers entwined and lightly pressed.

"From here you can almost see the whole county," Martha Hillyer said as they stopped at the very top while people were unloaded below.

"A whole world," the boy replied.

On the day before Angus MacLeod was to appear in court, Walter Johnston climbed the mountain in the gathering dusk. He measured the spot on the mountains where the sun set to the south of him. It was almost as far as it would go. November was about over. In a little more than three weeks the sun would set on its southernmost line for a few days, then start its slow but certain movement north again. Walking the earth, as he did, with time to look, to pause and see, Walter Johnston could have lived without a calendar— telling the month by the spot on the Blue Ridge where the sun rose and the line where it sank behind the Alleghenies.

As Angus and Walter Johnston talked before the fire, Tor found one excuse after another for not going to bed. Finally, he asked the question which he had been trying to get up courage enough to ask the whole evening: "Can I miss school and go to court with you tomorrow, Grandpa?"

"I think that would be very educational," Walter Johnston said before Angus had a chance to speak.

"If your grandmother thinks it's all right."

"She does. I've already asked her. Now I can go to bed."

"I haven't seen you to ask, how did the fair go this year, any prizes?" Walter Johnston asked as the boy rose to leave.

"For yearling Shorthorns, yes," the boy said. "For lambs nothing." Then a mumble from on the stairs, "The judges were partial to heavy mutton breeds, Hampshires and Southdowns."

"I would feel more at home in the county courthouse," Angus MacLeod said as they entered the great oak door of the judges' chambers in the town thirty miles up the valley.

Tor had expected a big courtroom, but what they entered was only a large room with a high ceiling and shelves of books on every side reaching to the top of the narrow windows. The books were all as big as the Bible at home, and all the covers were black or tan. A round white globe hung from the middle of the ceiling but did little to drive out the heavy gray of a sunless November day. The radiators rattled and steam whistled from the pipe at the end of one, but Tor felt cold.

There were narrow windows in pairs which reached from floor to ceiling. They came to a point like the ones at church. Tor wondered what scandalous remark his grandmother would make about them if she were there. She could never stand a dirty window. These hadn't been cleaned for so long that the cobwebs, their patterns plainly marked by black furnace dust, filled the corners of all the panes.

The only furniture in the room was two rows of heavy, hard-seated chairs facing a large table, behind which were three chairs. On the table there was a glass pitcher and three drinking glasses. The three tall-backed chairs behind the table had scrolls carved in the top of their backs. The rest of the backs were covered with black leather. The whole room had a musty smell, reminding Tor of the smell of moldy corncobs and rat droppings under the corncrib.

Tor studied the two closed doors on either side of the table at the front of the room. The large egg-shaped brass doorknobs remained fixed. Tor wished they would turn, release the latch, let the hinges whine under the weight of the tall doors, and that someone would come from the other side. Waiting seemed to give some unseen force more time to plot against his grandfather. Between the doors, on the wall behind the three tall chairs, there hung a picture of a man with a gray beard, wearing long black robes. The picture reached almost to the ceiling. In several places the gold was gone from the heavy frame and what looked like plain white plaster showed underneath.

Tor thought Angus looked very lonely. But there seemed to be nothing to say. He wished his grandfather would get up and pace up and down, the way he did at home sometimes when he was aggravated about something. He wondered if Angus was afraid of what was going on behind the tall doors with the egg-shaped brass knobs. He wished he had gone more often with Angus as he went up and down the mountain with his petitions, begging people to sign, having doors slammed in his face.

Finally, after what seemed to be forever to Tor, the door on the left side of the room opened and three black-robed men entered. None of them looked like the picture over the chairs, but one with a sheaf of unfolded papers in his hands looked almost as old, except that he didn't have a beard. All three seemed to be stoop-shouldered. Tor thought it might just be the robes, the way they hung.

Angus stood when the judges entered. Tor followed quickly when he saw his grandfather get up. Walter Johnston moved back from where he had been gazing through a dirt-clouded window out upon the deserted courthouse square. He took his place in front of a chair next to Angus.

"You may be seated," the judge who carried the papers said as he seated himself in the middle chair. His voice was soft, and Tor thought he detected traces of a smile kindle above the spectacles which sat far down on his nose.

"Which of you is Mr. Angus MacLeod?" the same judge asked as he lifted a page of the papers he had placed before him on the table and adjusted his spectacles upward. The two black-robed associates sat on either side, almost statue-like, Tor thought.

"I am Angus MacLeod, your Honor," Angus replied after he had risen again.

"You may sit, Mr. MacLeod. This is not a criminal court."

"Thank you, sir."

"Mr. MacLeod, the provisions of the law of eminent domain, of which you have been made aware previously, give the separate agencies of government—local, state, or federal—the right to acquire property for the public good. By the provisions of this law your property has been condemned by court order and appraised by duly appointed court appraisers.

"The question before this panel of three appellate court judges is whether or not you have been treated fairly. We sit merely to determine whether or not the value arrived at for your property, by duly appointed court appraisers, is fair and equitable. If the records before us show that the provisions of the law of eminent domain have been carried out properly and in your best interest and that of the public, then it is the duty of this court to decide a reasonable period of time for you to comply with the law by signing over your property for value received, and removing all chattel goods and properties from the premises. Do you understand?"

"I do, your Honor."

Tor liked the kindly way the judge spoke, but it seemed to him that there wasn't going to be much chance for Angus and Walter Johnston to argue against having to sell the farm. Part of the language was confusing, but the part about moving everything off the premises presented a picture completely new to Tor.

He had pictured change, yes, but never everything gone. His grandfather had talked some about trees, houses, hills being torn up, burned, moved—once the dreaded machines got started; but now for the first time that picture swam in the blur of heat waves, rising off the rattling radiator, before Tor's eyes. He began to feel sick from the heat.

How could everything be moved? He'd thought of moving sheep and cattle, that would be easy. But how would you move the great stone watering trough? And gates and neat stone walls? The giant flat stone at the kitchen door and the young apple trees that Tor had helped his grandfather plant the first year he lived at the farm? Some things just aren't meant to be moved.

Tor swallowed hard as he sat up straighter in his chair. He hoped he wouldn't have to go to the bathroom.

The judge continued, "The affidavit of the appraisers affirms that you had no objection to the price offered for your property. It further states that you refused to sign a contract to sell. And it also states that you offered no reason for not signing, except to say that your property was not for sale. Is that correct?"

"That is correct, sir," Angus answered after he had risen.

"Then the function of this panel, to serve as referees to approve or disapprove the values arrived at by due process of law, is complete. The three of us have made a careful study of the affidavits here presented." The judge lifted the sheaf of papers and shook them pointedly toward Angus. "So neither we nor you find fault with the assessment."

The judge was not speaking as softly now as when he began. Tor noticed that Angus' face got its aggravated look when the judge shook the papers. He did not sit down again either, and he looked much older to Tor than he had ever looked before. He was not standing up straight the way he always did. Now he was bent forward with his hands on the empty chair in the row in front of him. Tor wondered if Angus didn't feel sick too—the way he did. Tor thought he must feel cold too; he hadn't taken off his Mackinaw. Tor also picked up the sound of his bootheels tapping the floor as they did on the hearthstone when Angus rose from his rocker and stood aggravated before the fire.

"Is there anything you wish to say before we adjourn, Mr. MacLeod? The writ of mandamus, stating the date on or before which the property must be made available to the Federal Highway Commissioner, will be issued to you in due time. Consideration will be made as to crops stored, seasonal fluctuation as to value of livestock and machinery, et cetera, in case your plans include an auction."

The heel tapping had stopped. The tall mountain man, now bent as though facing into a mighty and relentless mountain blizzard, had lost his way. There was no right direction left to go. He fingered the buttons on his Mackinaw and loosed them one by one.

"All I want to say is that there's something awful wrong about a law that can destroy a man's whole life. If anybody cared, they could still look and see that it would make sense to build the road from Humpstack Gap to Fisher's Rock and not destroy my home. My inheritance that was to be my sons' inheritance. But they died in the war. And now it was to be my grandson's inheritance. But no one has ever talked about anything except appraisal, value, price. If something is not for sale, I've always said, it doesn't have a price." By the time he had finished speaking the mountain man was standing tall again. Now he sat down.

There was a general shuffling of papers and whispering among the three judges as they leaned together.

One studied a paper from the sheaf of pages and passed it among the others. Angus MacLeod sat with his shoulders bent, looking at the floor. Walter Johnston looked out past the windows, too filmed with dirt and cobwebs to let the yellowed globe light out or the dull sunless November day in.

Tor studied the three judges and the pitcher of water which no one had touched. His stomach was growing more squeamish by the minute. He thought a drink of water might help.

He felt ashamed because he had planned in his own mind how everything would work out to make his mountain dream world the way he wanted it. He felt guilty and numb because he had always thought Angus was really sort of stubborn and foolish, making too much of the whole thing.

Now suddenly the words of the judge—"a set time the property must be made available"—had produced a different picture. The judge's words meant the end—the end of the world that Tor MacLeod and Angus MacLeod had both loved, each in his own way.

He wished Walter Johnston would get up and shake his finger at the judges and say something. He wished there was something his grandfather could do—like kicking the chair in front of him out of the way, jerking the papers off the table, and throwing them in the wicker wastepaper basket that stood over against the wall.

He thought he'd stand up and tell the judges all the things that couldn't be moved—the great fireplace in the kitchen with the marks where his grandmother had measured how much his father and Uncle Logan grew each year when they were boys. The farm bell—would it ever sound right without its echo bouncing off the Hanging Gardens?

Finally the huddle ended, and the center judge began to speak. "We feel, Mr. MacLeod, that we need to consult your county agricultural agent as to the time for release of property and moving of all chattel goods which would cause you the least hardship. In the spring; but as to the exact date, you will receive our decision in due time. And as of this day, November 27, you are enjoined from planting any crop, such as wheat, oats, rye, barley or any other, whose harvest would delay occupation of the land by the Federal Highway Commissioner beyond the date of May fifteenth of next year."

Tor noticed that the judge was speaking softly again. When the three arose, the one who had presided came and shook hands with Angus. Tor didn't hear exactly what he said. He was suddenly aware that everything important had already been said.

❧ Thirteen ❧

In summer Una MacLeod went to the mailbox and always had the mail for Angus to look at when he took a short breather in his rocker on the porch before dinner. In winter Angus went to the mailbox, usually just when it arrived, or always before noontime.

After the day in court, Tor, who always looked in the mailbox when he got off the school bus out of curious habit, found the mail still there. He also noticed that after he had carried it to the house, Angus left it unnoticed on the kitchen table, sometimes not even reading the paper.

Then there came the day when Tor had to carry the dreaded court letter into the house. He gave it to his grandmother. She turned it in her hands several times and then said in her quiet way, "The court letter's come. Want me to open it?"

"Might as well," Tor's grandfather replied without taking his gaze off the log spitting in the fireplace.

After a few legal terms, Una MacLeod's voice began to quiver and go out. The date, May 15, was the last words she managed before she passed the letter to Tor.

Tor studied where she had left off. There was only one sentence left. He felt sick again like he had been at the courthouse. But he swallowed and read aloud, "Failure to comply with the provisions herein ordered will result in immediate forced evacuation from premises and contempt charges in the Third District Court of Appeals, Commonwealth of Virginia."

"We could be finished long before that," Angus MacLeod said after a long silence. "There won't be anything this year to make spring busy."

When Tor changed his boots and said to Shep, "Let's go to chores, boy," without first asking, "What's to eat?" Una MacLeod didn't ask her usual question, "Don't you feel well, Tor?" She knew his feeling.

"The middle of May, May fifteenth, May fifteenth," Tor said to himself as he walked toward the corncrib. How different spring would be. Calves and lambs would be born. But they'd have to be sold before they ever grew to race the pasture walls and leap its brook, if the auction came in early spring.

Angus' walking plow would turn no more brown furrows for robins to follow. Angus would not stretch his tired muscles and say, "The corn ground's ready, and if we have another week of warm days, the oak leaves will be big as a squirrel's ear and we can plant."

Tor stood in the corncrib door and looked back at the house. The low winter sun reflected against Una MacLeod's clean windows turned the ones facing west to gold. Suddenly the boy knew why Angus would not sell them to the man from Fredericksburg to restore James Monroe's law office. Maybe, Tor thought, he could save a lot of things, even the windows, when the house was wrecked, and Mr. Hillyer would let him put them in the old MacLean house. Nobody would buy Angus' walking plow; he might put it there too.

He felt weak inside, and it took several extra turns of the crank before the corn sheller got up speed enough for the balance wheel to keep it going. He shelled corn for the horses too old to eat it off the cob that Angus pampered in their old age, because they had earned their rest. Sometimes Tor had silently questioned his grandfather's wisdom in such quaint, staid practice. Now, thinking of the fate of these poor creatures, he was ashamed.

Angus MacLeod was not going to be hurried now. "We'll wait for May for the auction. By then all the lambs and calves, except those born late to first-bred ewes and heifers, will be old enough to wean if they're separated from their mothers by the sale."

"But don't you want to change your mind and buy another farm?" Tor asked as they talked several days after the letter had come. He had heard his grandmother and Walter Johnston ask the same question. Tor got the same short answer he had heard them get: "No. I'm too old. My heart wouldn't be in the land."

It was about seed catalog time, about the time when Angus would think of walking his fields in winter, that he and Una MacLeod went down the mountain to the courthouse and signed away their survivorship deed that had been passed down from MacLeod and heirs to MacLeod and heirs since the year 1782.

The lawyers for the Federal Highway Commission and the National Park Service had not been able to find a registration for the MacLeod cemetery. They questioned its existence.

"When was the law made that they had to be registered?" Angus asked in reply to a statement of one of the lawyers that no private cemetery was registered in the name of MacLeod.

"Not until some time after the War Between the States," one of the lawyers replied, "when the law was passed that all burials had to be recorded —white and black. The same law required public cemeteries to provide a pauper's field for burial of the poor."

"Then the MacLeod cemetery had been going nearly a hundred years before the law. No wonder it was never registered. The law says it can't be sold and it can't be violated. I guess that means it can't be dug up or have concrete laid over it."

"That's correct, Mr. MacLeod; but without either registration or gravestones, as the surveyors' report indicates, we need proof that it exists and did exist prior to requirement for registration."

"There's the Bible, Angus," Una MacLeod said quietly.

"Yes! There's the old Bible." Angus' voice showed that his patience was acquiring a jagged edge. "In it is a diagram of graves' locations, names, dates of birth and death. The first entry is Unnamed Infant, aged three days, 1784. That would be the second year after the first MacLeod took his bride to a log cabin atop the mountain.

The last entries are 1944, two, Captain Torm MacLeod and Lieutenant Logan MacLeod. They were killed in the war. Reported within a week of each other. Is that proof enough?"

"I'm sorry, Mr. MacLeod, but sometimes legal matters seem a little too particular and demanding to the average person. We'll have to make a copy of the page you refer to and have it notarized as a true copy."

Two days later Angus carried the great Bible into the courthouse. When the photographing and notarizing were finished, he went by to visit his friend Judge Garber.

"You're taking the holy word to the streets?" the judge asked with a smile when he saw the Bible.

"No, I just had to prove that MacLeods do die and there is a cemetery where they're buried. And believe me, I had a hard time proving it."

The winter did not drag with its heavy silence as slowly as Tor had thought it would. He marveled that Angus bothered to put new gate slats in all the gates that needed them. One day, as spring approached, when he came home from school, Angus proudly announced, "I walked the walls today. Put back all the stones that the frost or some critter had loosened."

There were other things new to Angus and Una MacLeod which used up the time he would have been plowing and planting. They went into the valley to find a house. Angus MacLeod said it should be at the edge of the town, not in it. Una MacLeod wanted it to have a dining room big enough to hold the MacLeod dining-room table that seated twenty people, whose top was a single piece of oak sawed from MacLeod timber and shaped by MacLeod hands. Both Angus and Una wanted a kitchen with a fireplace; both wanted the house to have a porch. But there was no house for sale with a dining room big enough for the MacLeod table, so they settled for one with a fireplace in the kitchen and a long porch.

Tor was busy too. He spent many Saturdays repairing fences at the old McLean place where Mr. Hillyer was going to care for his Cheviots and Shorthorn cattle.

"Why don't you come and live with us when your grandfather moves?" Martha Hillyer asked as they worked together.

"I am in the summer. But I'd hurt my mother if I did in winter."

As the date approached for the auction, Angus spent a lot of time going among the Mennonite farmers in the valley. He wanted to sell his animals into the best homes he could find, and there were none better than the Mennonites. And they came and looked and bought.

"I'll give you this team of chestnuts if you sign a paper to care for these two old horses that I've laid by, too old to work. . . . This cultivator's seen a lot of use, but it's still good. . . . I don't want any of my cows to go to the slaughterhouse. You can have them for the price of springing heifers."

"What's a springing heifer?" Tor interrupted.

"One that's calving for the first time," his grandfather answered, and went back to finding good homes for his animals. "There's not a better bloodline of Black-faced Highland sheep this side of

Dunvegan, Scotland. If they're auctioned off, who knows, they'll probably end up on a scrub farm over the mountains on the Seneca River or be scattered between backyard lots and butcher shops."

Six weeks before auction time Angus had sold almost all his animals. "Grandfather says that the Mennonites are the world's best farmers and managers," Tor said to his grandmother as he watched through the window as another man in his black clothes and broad-rimmed black hat took from his pocket a cloth money poke and began to count out bills to Angus. "But he's wrong. I think Grandpa is the world's best manager."

"He's straightened up a lot since he got the idea of selling to the Mennonites. This will make the last shock a little easier; better than seeing everything go at once. It'll be hard enough having strange walls to look at," Tor's grandmother said.

If Angus MacLeod was a man who had good ideas, ideas were also being stirred in the men who came up the mountain to buy from the man "who had to sell out," words that the Mennonites so dreaded ever coming true among their own or anyone else.

Milo Simons, from Singers Glen on the other side of the valley, had been one of the first who came to buy. Angus had given him the chestnut team in exchange for life care of the team too old for work. He had bought Angus' three other horses, including Little Sorrel, paid in cash, and gone away thinking he had more than a bargain.

Angus had agreed to feed the old horses until he had to get out. Milo Simons was about to pay the MacLeod farm a second visit. It would be a day like no other day Angus MacLeod could ever remember.

The day had begun badly. Tor, listening to Angus and Una talk the night before about things from the house that would have to be auctioned off because they wouldn't fit into the house in the valley, had gone to bed with it on his mind and had lived the whole fateful auction day in a dream.

Tor sat at the breakfast table, pale and troubled-looking.

"Are you sick?" his grandmother asked as she reached over and felt his forehead.

"No, I just dreamed what the auction will be like. It's only about six weeks away. There were people all over the place. It was real crazy at the start, but then it was just like the other two auctions I've been to—curious people looking into everything, wandering through the buildings and the house, picking up whatever has been left lying around.

"But when it started the auctioneer was out by the kitchen door calling for a bid on Grandmother's signal bell. The golden eagle from Hanging Gardens was soaring in a low circle over the people's heads and everybody was watching it, paying no attention to the auctioneer. Then he told you, Grandpa, to go get your gun and shoot that pesky bird, and you did.

"The eagle fell straight out of the sky and landed in the watering trough with a great splash. All the people laughed, and one man yelled, 'I'll give a dollar for the gun,' and another person yelled, 'A dollar fifty,' and the auctioneer said, 'Sold.' "

Una MacLeod was trying to catch the boy's eye to stop him. She said, "Eat your breakfast, please, Tor."

But he seemed not to hear.

"Then you said, 'No! Don't sell that gun,' and grabbed it. You took the gun and a rocker from the porch, called old Blue Boy and Tennessee Belle after you, and went and sat right in the gateway of the burying ground. And you sat there all day, looking toward the inside, not seeing what was happening at the auction."

"Tor," his grandmother pleaded laughingly, but not feeling that way, "haven't we had enough of that crazy dream?"

"Go on. I want to hear the end of this," Angus interrupted. "I'll probably feel just the way you found me in the dream. Except I'll go far out of hearing—up in the Indian mound pasture."

"Ladies from the church in town were selling sandwiches and coffee on the porch. One of them said, looking at you with the shotgun across your lap, 'He's addlebrained. Too bad. But . . . you can't stand in the way of progress.' Then the preacher, who was helping, spoke up and said, 'Progress means one thing to one person and something else to another.'

"One of the ladies said in a prissy way, 'Where is dear Mrs. McLeod? I want to ask if the pewter ware in the corner cupboard is going to be sold.' And someone walking out the door with the iron trivet that says 'God Bless Our Home' said, 'She's not here. The old man sent her to visit relatives in the city until this is all over.' "

"That's a very good idea; and it's exactly what we'll do. This dream of yours is full of good ideas," Angus said jokingly and added, "Better start getting packed, Mother. It's only six weeks and you don't take many trips. It'll take awhile for you to get ready."

"Some man bought the big oak dining-room table for four dollars. 'It'll make a great workbench,' he was telling one of his friends, and to show how strong it was, he took the big poker from the fireplace and hit down across the top as hard as he could. I was rubbing the smooth top with my hand to show that it was too good to be used for a workbench and the poker smashed all my fingers. The man just laughed and said, 'Keep your hands off that table, it belongs to me.' "

"Tor! The school bus will be along soon and you haven't eaten a bite," his grandmother pleaded.

"Then with my hand bleeding, I ran all the three miles down to Hillyers' farm. And by the time I got there it was summer and school was out. Martha Hillyer wrapped up my hand in a towel. When Mr. Hillyer saw it, he said, 'Boy, you're crippled. You can't work for me this summer.'

"That's when the dream ended."

"And there's the school bus," Angus said as he got up and held the boy's jacket.

When the boy was gone, Angus pretended to be

still amused by the boy's crazy dream. But both he and Una MacLeod knew the grim truth of it, slightly twisted in the boy's troubled mind, yet pictures too real to go away.

"Tor is more bothered by all this than he's let on," Una MacLeod said. "Maybe we did the wrong thing by keeping him here."

Angus did not answer; for it was just at this point he got up to look out of the window. There was the rattle of buggy wheels on the lane toward the barnyard.

"There's Milo Simons. He's the Mennonite I sold the horses to, and made a deal for him to care for the old ones. I guess he's changed his mind and doesn't want them." Angus pulled on his Mackinaw and went out.

Milo Simons had tied his horse to the gate. The two men met on the path to the kitchen. After the usual greeting, "Good day to you, brother," and idle talk of ground being ready to plant and good weather, Milo began, "I've been doing some thinking, Brother MacLeod."

Angus knew that the Mennonites called every man brother. This didn't mean that Milo hadn't changed his mind about the aged horses.

"And me and some of my people from Singers Glen and Linville, who came up to buy your stock and saw your place, have been talking."

"Let's go to the kitchen," Angus interrupted. "There's still a tail end of March chill dragging after April until the sun's been up half the morning."

In the kitchen, Una MacLeod hung Milo Simons' black hat on the rack and the two men took places at the long table where she had put two coffee cups.

"We Mennonites are all carpenters, you know, Brother MacLeod. The *One* we follow, and try to do *His* teaching, was a carpenter, too, you know. So we build our own houses, teach our young to follow the golden rule, help our neighbor when he needs us, care for our aged, and tend to our own business. That's the whole story in a nutshell.

"But what I came about is this. When we came to buy your stock and saw your place, the way somebody had built—"

"My forebears, going all the way back to 1782," Angus interrupted.

"I said to Amel Snider that it was a terrible sin for a house like this to be torn down to make way for a road."

"It is an awful criminal thing that the government's doing. I fought it every way I could, but I lost. We've lost what's been our whole life."

"Last night we met at Amel's place. He's about halfway between Singers Glen and Linville. Altogether there were thirty-two men and boys, and twelve others sent word. There have been letters written to friends in Pennsylvania, too. What we decided, Brother MacLeod, is this: If you can buy a piece of land somewhere, we want to come and move your house."

Una MacLeod had been shocked at Tor blurting out his strange dream, but that was nothing. Now she stopped her busy work around the stove, slumped in a chair and buried her face in her apron.

"I've always had considerable praise for you people," Angus said in a broken voice after a long silence. "I knew you always helped each other at barn raisings and when one of your people got burned out."

"We figure this way. If the weather holds, we'll be through planting in the next three weeks. After planting there's a little slack time when nothing is urgent. That would leave us three weeks before you have to get out.

"Could you buy a piece of land somewhere to your likin'?"

Angus thought a long time. When he spoke, it was as a man talking in his sleep. "Last year my neighbor down over the mountain, when he thought they would take my land, said he'd sell me a second farm he owned above his big one. But I never said anything about it. I was fighting in the courts and thought I would win. I never thought I would lose. But it's too late now. You're neighborly and mean well. But this house could never be moved. Besides, there's no time. It was a hundred years in building—to stand atop this mountain forever, I guess."

"There's time enough, Brother MacLeod. There's more than time enough. In Pennsylvania, Mercer County, around Grove City, when the Beaver River flooded and washed away seven houses and nine barns, we had the people back under their own roofs, storing harvests hauled in by neighbors in newly built barns, in six weeks. Eight years ago when a tornado tore through the upper Miami Valley in Shelby County, Ohio, you should have seen it. Seventeen school bus loads of men and boys from Virginia, Indiana, Pennsylvania, Ohio. The whole valley strewn with wreckage—looked like Ezekiel's valley of dry bones. We cleaned it up and built it back."

"But these were your people you were helping," Angus said. Because there seemed nothing else to say. And he knew he was wrong.

Milo Simons did not answer, but continued, "In Lycoming County, Pennsylvania, a power company condemned a man's property, like the government did yours, to run a high tension line. The line went right over a stone barn—eighty-five feet long, forty-five feet wide, and forty feet high to the peak of the roof. The owner had been paid enough to build a new barn. But not like that one! Ten days before the bulldozers and cranes were to clear it out of the way and bury the stone, three hundred Mennonites moved in and eight days later it had been carried, stone by stone, to a new foundation three hundred yards from the power line, the distance the regulations required.

"Your house would be so easy to move. Take it down log by log, numbered, and they'd go right back in place. Lot of paneling inside that would go right back in place. Only thing new would be a little plastering."

"Look at the stones in that fireplace, and these beams," Angus said, pointing to the ceiling, "all pegged together."

"We've got friends in Lancaster County, Pennsylvania, who can lay a chimney faster than the mortar can set. They do plumbing and electrical work while the cement sets up. And a pegged building is the easiest to dismantle and put back together. There's little chalk marks that nobody understands but the one who put them there. But when he points and says, 'That beam and them two braces go there,' they do. Pegs don't make any difference; they're all for the same size hole. Our boys each stand ready with an armful of different lengths. When somebody yells, 'Ten-inch peg,' he better have a free hand, for the boy's already twirled it."

Angus sat motionless, speechless, and exhausted. Just listening to Milo Simons made him feel as though he'd come from a hard day in the fields.

Una MacLeod had regained sufficient self-control to hold up her head and smooth out the damp spots, left by silent tears, on her apron. To her it was like one of Tor's games when he was younger and would come running to her and say, "Guess what I just thought up?"

Una MacLeod was a good judge of human nature. Now she sat stunned and puzzled. A total stranger, at least to her, from the valley, twelve miles away, had left home at seven o'clock in the morning to make the trip in his buggy, had said your house is fine carpentry; the *One* we try to follow was a carpenter; we will take down your house and move it for you. Could this be true?

"It's quite a sight to see a bunch of black-frocked monkeys, thick as ants on a dry pine log, climbing over a building." With a soft smile Milo Simons spoke to Una MacLeod; her bewilderment and doubt had not gone unnoticed.

Now the three laughed together.

"It would be a real frolic for us," Milo Simons

said as he left, looking at the house. "You'd have to buy new wood shingles for the kitchen wing, and we might split a few molding strips inside, but other than new pipes, wiring, and foundation, you'd have no cost."

"You couldn't save that slate roof?" And once again Angus felt he had said the wrong thing.

"Every single slate! Start at the top and peel 'em off, like feathers off a molting hen. And a line from roof to ground like ants passing bread crumbs."

"It would be a miracle." Angus stood fixed, gazing back at the house.

"You could get big machinery in to do the foundation. It would be ready by the time we have our seed in the ground. Think about it, Brother MacLeod. You'll have to bring me word. I don't have a telephone. Let me know as soon as you can. We've got some neighbors in Pennsylvania and Ohio who'll want to know," Milo Simons called back as he slapped the lines against the sleek flanks of a horse he addressed with "Home, Rick," and was off at a brisk trot.

In the kitchen Una wiped her tears and said, "Could it be?"

"Might well be!" Angus spoke with his old spirit again. "A dream that'll knock Tor's dream of auction day into a cocked hat."

"But we've already bought that house in the valley."

"No matter. We can rent it. Best thing to do with the money we get from the government is to buy property. If Hillyer will still sell me the old McLean place, we'll own it before chore time.

Last year he offered. Said I could have the whole place. About a hundred acres. I'm going to see him right now."

"But that's a lot of land when you said you could never put your heart in any other land."

"For the boy! Something to leave for Tor. Hillyer will sell. I might not be back till near chore time. We'll go straight to Judge Garber and have him draw a deed. If he won't sell, I might try on down the mountain."

Una MacLeod had not seen the man step as briskly for so long she could not remember when. The great stockage kitchen door closed after him with its living vibration once again. It shook the cups on their hooks in the cupboard. Even the house seemed to know it was coming to life again.

Angus MacLeod passed the stakes on the road where the government parkland would end. Below them was Hillyers' upper fields, what had once been the McLean farm.

"Since I talked to you last year when this first happened, things have changed some," David Hillyer, Senior, said as he and Angus leaned on a gate looking up from Hillyers' farm proper to the McLean place. "I've sort of promised it to another buyer. There is a problem, though. He wants me to hold it for twenty years or so. And in between now and then he wants to use it rent free to raise Cheviot sheep and Shorthorn cattle."

David Hillyer couldn't hold in his laughter any longer.

Then he was serious again. Angus listened in silence. "That boy has been awful torn up about having to leave this mountain. He's a lot different from kids I know. Take for example, he's asked me if he can use the old McLean house to store some things he wants to keep from the farm: the farm bell, your mailbox, the big flat stone by the kitchen door; has asked me if I'll take my tractor up and haul it down at the right time. He's got a whole list—too long for me to remember."

When the two men had reached an agreement, they shook hands.

"No use for me to go to the judge's office," David Hillyer said. "You can give him the details."

Judge Garber bit his cigar almost in half and chewed it into fragments as he listened to Angus' story. When Angus had finished, the judge said, "Well, I'll tell you, those Mennonites are bad people to do business with, bad for *me*, that is. If everybody was like them, I wouldn't have a job; they never get involved with the law.

"Why, they don't even buy insurance! Faith and their neighbors is all the insurance they ever need. How do you want this property title to read on the deed?"

"MacLeod and heirs, forever."

"That's not legal. It has to be MacLeod and heirs in perpetuity. Means the same thing as forever but sounds more complicated; so I can charge more for writing it."

Angus was back home, having gone without dinner, before school bus time.

He walked with Shep to wait by the mailbox.

When the bus came, he watched the boy let one boot fall heavily after the other down the steps to the ground. The wide strides that skipped whole steps and almost outreached a boy's balance in April mud were gone. Even Shep wagged his tail halfheartedly because his master's greeting was little more than a grunt.

Someone in the bus knocked on the window and waved. The boy swung his books halfheartedly in that direction.

"Those young apple trees we planted several years ago have buds. They'll bloom this year," Angus said as he pointed.

"But they'll never live to bear fruit," the boy answered. "The bulldozers will probably get them."

"They're still young enough to be moved though."

"But where?" the boy asked. "That yard at the new house wouldn't hold them."

"I thought you might want to ask Mr. Hillyer if you could move them down to the old McLean place. It's a pity for them to be destroyed. He could bring his tractor with the front-end shovel, lift them out, and haul them down on his flat-bedded tractor cart."

"I've already asked him too much," the boy said after he had thought for a long time. "He might get annoyed if I ask any more."

When Tor had spread his soup, his bread and meat, before him on the table, Angus looked at Una and said, "You tell him, Mother?"

"I can't. You'll have to." She raised her apron to her eyes, and Tor stopped eating.

"Remember that time over near Bridgewater, we stopped and watched those Mennonites putting up the timbers for a barn, how the siding was going on at the same time the roof sheathing was, and you said they'd have it ready for hay before dark—roof and all. And you counted about fifty men and boys, with eight or ten girls carrying cold lemonade or water to the men. It was some sight."

"What's happened? Our barn didn't burn."

"No. But I have a better dream than the one you told us at breakfast. Listen to this. Milo Simons, the Mennonite who's going to get the old horses, drove up in his buggy this morning. He said the people who'd come up to buy stock thought it would be an awful sin for this house to be destroyed. He and his neighbors want to move it."

"Whole! That's impossible."

"No, piece by piece. Said they moved a big stone barn in Pennsylvania, stone by stone, and put it on a new foundation in eight days, or maybe less."

"Where to? On their land down in the valley?"

"No. We bought some land today; the old McLean place from Mr. Hillyer. Now you won't have to work out the rent—" Angus didn't finish because a chair fell over backward, Shep barked when he was tripped over, the door slammed, the boy and dog were gone.

Angus and Una MacLeod would argue later about the order in which things happened: "He went down on his hands and knees yelling," Angus said, "and kissed the flat stone by the kitchen door, and smoothed it with his hands like it was a velvet carpet."

"No, he first rang the bell," Una MacLeod said, "until the whole mountain shook and I thought that bell would crack for sure. Then he hugged the bell post.

"He went through the orchard and touched every young tree we had planted together," Una remembered.

"He cleared the barnyard gate with only one hand on the top slat. By the time I got out to the barn he was climbing out of my ornery rams' pen. Had climbed in by mistake; thought he was in the next pen where his Cheviots with lambs were. The rams helped him out in a hurry."

"Then he went up to his room, four steps at a time," Una said. "He had to be called for supper. That wasn't like him at all. When he came down, it was one step at a time, very slowly. I thought he'd hurt himself in his wild cavorting. After supper he said he'd had such a terrible day at school he'd missed a couple of assignments. He'd have to go down and get them from Martha Hillyer. When he went out the door, I said to Angus he ought to drive him down, so he could get back and do his studies. And Angus said, 'He won't be back till ten o'clock. This just ain't the day for book learnin'.' "

The third week in April the foundation was ready, in the highest field, just a few hundred feet from a spring. From here one still looked far out over the valley westward to the Alleghenies.

When the mellow-brown, stoneless fields of the Mennonite farmers were planted, these brotherly people came: Milo Simons, Amel Snider, Rufus

Wampler, and a hundred and forty more besides, seventy one week and another seventy the next.

From the valley, twelve heavy flatbed wagons, some with an extra team hitched aft, some with a third horse, pulling tandem. From Pennsylvania a school bus load of men and boys arriving on a Saturday morning at dawn, unpacking tents and stoves, toolboxes filled with polished saws, chisels, wrecking bars, and hammers with their homemade handles; jugs of cider, long loaves of bread, brick-sized squares of pan scrapple, sides of beef and hams already cooked. Friendly greetings all around and laughter; "a picnic or a carnival," a passerby would have said.

Hayfork ropes and ladders, pulleys and heavy chains, stout timbers and rough-sawed boards for scaffolding, and everywhere the touch of skill. Braces and timbers hoisted on a wagon made a movable scaffold.

Women drove up from the valley to cook and spread the long board table, laid out on sawhorses in the tents. Men pulled their blue, brown, or white bib overalls over their dark suits for working, but took them off when they entered the tent to eat.

Boys stood spaced on ladders and scaffolding, their wide-brimmed hats always on their heads, and passed slate shingles, sheathing boards, chimney stones, wooden pegs from beams down to be loaded on the waiting wagons.

The long wagons were loaded with logs, all numbered with carpenter's chalk and lifted gently out of their places, then let down by ropes and pulleys. When the load was high enough, the driver, leaning against the lines to hold a restless four-horse team, would call out, "That's it for this load." Off he would go, wheels whining under the heavy load, down to where other men waited, who read the chalked numbers and lifted each log back into its proper place, always accompanied by friendly laughter, the ring of busy hammers, and boys humming the hymn "Lead Kindly Light" as they twirled pegs to men fitting beam and brace together.

"You should have hurried over here when I wrote," Angus MacLeod said to his friend Walter Johnston, who had stopped overnight on one of his walking trips.

They were rocking on the same long porch, the rockers creaking on the same flagstone floor. Angus pointed out a few dim chalk marks and numbers.

"Every stone put back in place. You should have been here. You could write a book about it.

"I could sit here and rock a hundred years and I still couldn't tell it all. And if I told it a hundred times, you would still have to see it to believe it."

"The barn and all the other buildings, too. You didn't write me that."

"Didn't know it myself till they started loosing the timbers. I told Milo Simons they'd already done too much, that I wasn't going to do much except let Tor have his stock, that we didn't need it. But they moved it anyway.

"I tried to give them money. It was worth more than a body could ever say or pay, and I'd been paid well for my land. When I brought it up, Rufus Wampler, one of the leaders and a good stonemason said, 'If we took cash from you, we'd never be able to get credit from the Lord.'"

"How long were they at it altogether?" Walter Johnston asked.

"Twelve working days and two extra days for stonemasons rebuilding the chimneys.

"Only one accident on the whole job. Rufus Wampler was working on the chimney, sneezed, and his false teeth flew out, dropped down the chimney and broke in half. One of the boys stopped mixing mortar, passed his hat among the workers, and pushed a hat full of bills in Rufus' bib overall pockets. Amel Snider called up laughing and said, 'Now, Rufus, you can go somewhere besides Sears and Roebuck and get your teeth this time.'"

"And you had time left over till the deadline for being out?"

"Plenty! Tor and I took Hillyer's tractor with the front-end loader and moved all the young apple trees Tor and I had planted."

"You using a tractor! I wish I'd seen that."

"No, the boy. I found out he's been driving Hillyer's since before he could reach the pedals."

The laughter of the men shut out the deep boom of distant blasting, which rolled like thunder down from the mountaintop. Or if they heard it, neither took notice. Their laughter drowned out, too, the voices of a boy and girl calling to each other from the far corners of a field where lambs played follow-the-leader in and out among their grazing mothers.

The blasts which shook the mountain tore away the cliffs where pine and laurel grew in crevices— the cliffs an old man had named the Hanging Gardens. Slab after slab of cliffs split off and crashed in clouds of dust. Jagged scars and pointed edges stuck up against the sky. Wind and rain, frost, sleet and snow must start again and work ten thousand years to make them smooth.

Giant blades and gouging mouths of huge earthmovers chewed the green sod from fields where once a man had quickened his pace to follow April to his highest pasture. The bulldozers would have made a game of pushing a great flat stone that stood before a kitchen door into the gaping cellar hole, but levers handled gently and with skill had moved the stone away. So the bulldozers amused themselves by tearing out the roots of an ancient maple tree and burying stone walls which had stood a hundred years. Water spurted from underground as deep wounds were opened in the land.

A curious driver raised his blade and backed away. He called a friend to see. "Look!" he yelled above the roar of trucks grinding deep ruts as they passed. "Some poor damn fool built conduits of stone underground and made a field out of a swamp."

"Think of all that work," his friend yelled back.

Near where some giant sycamore trees had held a bank against a swirling stream, now there were only stumps. A driver, watching his twelve-ton load of earth and rock plunge down to fill what was once a boy's swimming hole, picked three arrowheads from the earth as it passed. No one had bothered to save the Indian mound where the council house had stood.

And when the blasting ends for the day and the machines cough out their last heavy smoke and are quiet, there is silence. The bobwhites, the meadowlarks and the bobolinks have gone to sing in other fields.

The boy and girl, calling to each other across the field, meet where a brook winds toward the lowland. They stand and watch a crayfish frantically burying itself in the clean gravel at the bottom of the brook.

"Why is it doing that?" the girl asks.

"Creature wisdom, Grandpa says," the boy answered, "feels the vibrations of the earth from the blasting and seeks a safer place. Like land turtles leave the lowland when there's going to be a flood."

"Tor," the girl asked, "do you believe in dreams?"

"Only after they've come true."

"That's a silly answer. Wanta walk up the mountain and watch the blasting?"

"No. Let's walk through all the fields until we find where the brook begins. There'll be a mountain spring with ferns growing, and deep shade, and a hermit thrush singing to itself. Grandpa says that's where they always nest."

The boy reached out his hand to help the girl to his side of the brook. Still holding hands, they went on together.

So I saw that there is nothing better
Than that a man should enjoy his work,
For that is his lot;
Who can bring him to see
What will be after him
—Ecclesiastes 3:22

This earth, this time, this life, are
stranger than a dream.
—THOMAS WOLFE,
The Hills Beyond

About the Author

Sounder, William H. Armstrong's first novel for young readers, won the distinguished Newbery Award. His subsequent books, *Sour Land* and *Barefoot in the Grass: The Story of Grandma Moses*, have also been highly acclaimed.

Mr. Armstrong was born and reared on a farm in the Shenandoah Valley near Lexington, Virginia. There he developed his lifelong interest in history and his abiding love for the land.

After graduation from Hampden-Sydney College, Mr. Armstrong began his teaching career while attending graduate school at the University of Virginia. He now teaches history at the Kent School and has written a number of books on education, in addition to his novels.

Mr. Armstrong lives in a house he designed and built for himself and his family on Skiff Mountain, overlooking the Housatonic River in Connecticut. The beautiful surrounding landscape is kept well tended by his flock of Corriedale sheep.